HOME FROM HOME

**Produced by the
Information Services Department, Central Bureau,
Seymour Mews House, Seymour Mews,
London W1H 9PE**

First edition

This guide is published by the Central Bureau, the UK national office responsible for the provision of information and advice on all forms of educational visits and exchanges; the development and administration of a wide range of curriculum related pre-service and in-service exchange programmes; the linking of educational establishments and local education authorities with counterparts abroad; and the organisation of meetings and conferences related to professional international experience.

Its information and advisory services extend throughout the educational field. In addition, over 20,000 individual enquiries are received and answered each year. Publications cater for the needs of people of all ages seeking information on the various opportunities available for educational contacts and travel abroad.

The Central Bureau was established in 1948 by the British government and is funded by the Department of Education & Science, the Scottish Education Department and the Department of Education for Northern Ireland.

Chairman of the Board: JG Evans, Director of Education, Derbyshire

Director: AH Male

Deputy Director: JP Carpenter

Distributed by the Central Bureau, Seymour Mews, London W1H 9PE, England Telephone 01-486 5101 Telex 21368 CBEVEX G

ISBN 0 900087 77 3

Typeset, printed and bound in England by David Green Printers Ltd, Kettering, Northamptonshire

The Central Bureau

Seymour Mews House, Seymour Mews, London W1H 9PE Tel 01-486 5101
3 Bruntsfield Crescent, Edinburgh EH10 4HD Tel 031-447 8024

16 Malone Road, Belfast BT9 5BN Tel 0232-6641/9

CONTENTS

7 USING THE GUIDE

HOMESTAYS: MAINLAND EUROPE

HOMESTAYS: BRITAIN, IRELAND & CHANNEL ISLANDS

TERM STAYS

PRACTICAL INFORMATION

REPORT FORM

USING THE GUIDE

Using the guide Before organising any homestay, exchange or term stay, it is important to consider carefully exactly what can be gained from the experience. A homestay involves being welcomed into a home in another country and being treated as a member of the family and the local community. You will learn about the family's attitudes and values by taking part in their day-to-day routine and activities, improving your language ability and vocabulary, and become involved in the life of the local community. In theory a homestay is strictly one-way, but in practice participants often find that their compatibility with their hosts is such that the homestay develops into an exchange, the foreign partner visiting them in their own home at some stage in the future. An exchange operates on much the same basis as a homestay, the difference being that hospitality received will be repaid in kind when the exchange partner is welcomed into your own home. This may take place consecutively, your partner accompanying you on your journey home, or can be delayed until the next holiday period, or even the following year. The matching procedure for exchanges is particularly important and every care should be taken to ensure that you provide as accurate a picture of yourself, and as much time as possible so that a suitable exchange partner can be found. A term stay involves attending a foreign school for one term or longer, and can operate either on a homestay or exchange basis. It is an extremely good way of finding out about life in a particular country as one becomes totally immersed not just in family life, but in school and community life as well. Many organisations offer term stays in the United States, where for British citizens at least the language is not likely to present a problem. If, however, you propose to take part in a term stay in a country whose language is not your own, you will need to have an adequate command of the language to cope not only with everyday life but with learning in the classroom. Visits, whether homestays, termstays or exchanges can be demanding. You will need to be open to what may seem to be a totally different culture, willing to accept new values and customs, to adapt to the lifestyle of your host family, and to cope with the difficulties of being surrounded by people speaking a foreign language. The time it takes to set up a homestay or exchange may vary considerably, but generally speaking it takes longer to arrange an exchange since the matching procedure is of major importance. Whatever type of stay you choose, you should ideally allow a period of 2-3 months so that the agency or organisation can find a suitable host family and make all the necessary arrangements. Some organisations insist on a longer period of time; the more notice you are able to give the organisation, particularly for exchanges, the better your chances of having a successful stay. As there are more people wishing to learn English than there are British people wanting to learn foreign languages, exchange applicants from mainland Europe may have to wait some time for an exchange partner to be found, and may therefore find it more convenient to take part in a homestay. Once you have decided on the country you wish to visit, and have been in touch with a suitable agency or organisation, you should read their literature and application forms very thoroughly. Make sure that you know exactly what is covered by the basic fee, for example, what type of insurance cover, if any, is provided, what the escorted travel arrangements are, and what provisions are made for

illnesses or accidents, or for returning home if serious difficulties should arise. If there are any points at all which are unclear, or if you have any other queries, you should contact the agency to receive clarification. It is obviously wise to have a clear idea of the procedure well before you actually apply. Further information and applications should be addressed to the organisations direct, and not to the Central Bureau.

In this guide information on the agencies and organisations arranging homestays, exchanges and term stays has been provided in a set format:

Individuals, groups or families
Many of the organisations listed in addition to arranging opportunities for individuals can also arrange stays for groups and families. The following symbols at the top of each entry show whether the organisation caters for individuals, groups, and/or families:

Individuals

Groups

Families

Profile Each agency or organisation listed is of a bona fide status and a general description of the nature of each organisation is given here together with its main field of activity, its foundation date and its status - commercial, private or charitable.

Areas Some organisations concentrate or specialise on particular cities or areas; others have contacts throughout a particular country. Most are able to arrange stays with families in a variety of areas, both urban and rural. As much information as possible regarding location has been provided in the entries, but it is always worth contacting individual organisations if you have a preference for an area which is not specifically mentioned. Sometimes you will be able to specify a preference when you apply, but it is important to remember that the first priority for a successful homestay or exchange is to find a suitable host family, and so you may not necessarily be offered a stay in the area of your choice. In the case of an exchange, insisting on a specific area may severely reduce the number of potential partners.

Matching By far the most important factor on an exchange holiday is to have the most compatible partner and host family. Exchange entries give details of the matching procedure, and all the exchange organisations listed here put a strong emphasis on this, particularly in the case of young people, and will make every effort to make a successful match. However the success of an exchange depends on the agency being provided with full background information on the exchange partners. Prospective exchange partners should take considerable care and effort in completing an exchange application form, and give the fullest details on their interests and background. Whilst a few organisations do try to meet participants personally, the majority depend entirely on the information provided on the application form to make a match.

Ages The age ranges catered for by a particular organisation is always indicated in the entry. Most organisations specialise in arranging stays for certain age groups, but some have no particular restrictions. Generally speaking, homestays are open to those aged 8-80, although most are in the 14-21 age range. There are few organisations which actually specialise in exchanges or visits for adults.

Stay Details of the usual length of stays and time of year when the stays operate are stated. The average homestay or exchange generally lasts 2-3 weeks, but many organisations are able to arrange shorter or longer stays according to individual requirements. Term stays can last from one term to a full academic year.

Level of language/English required Many organisations prefer participants to have at least a basic knowledge of the language of the country they plan to visit. Even where this is not specified, you should make a point of indicating your knowledge of the relevant language when applying. If you have no knowledge of the language, you should if you are to get the most out of your stay, and as a matter of courtesy, try and learn at least a little of the everyday vocabulary.

Language tuition Many organisations arrange language courses for participants; this is either inclusive in the programme, or may be arranged at extra cost.

Activities Some organisations include excursions and activities in the stay, while others arrange leisure activities at extra cost. Always check this beforehand with the organisation concerned. Most host families are only too happy to include the visitor in their activities, and to make a special effort to arrange visits. Check with the organisation to find out whether you are required to pay additional costs such as entrance fees, or whether allowance has already been made for this in your payment.

Cost Wherever possible, the full cost of the homestay or exchange programme has been quoted. Unless otherwise indicated costs quoted generally include the basic fee paid to the agency to cover administrative costs, and meals, accommodation and usually travel and insurance. Prices vary depending on the facilities the host family is able to offer, and the type of board provided. Where additional costs are involved, for example for insurance, excursions, escorted travel or school fees, this is indicated.

Accommodation This is usually arranged in a single or twin-bedded room. Some families may not be able to offer single rooms, and if you object to sharing a room your choice may therefore be more limited. Many organisations insist that only one visitor will be placed with a particular family at a time, ensuring that guests get good opportunity to practise the foreign language whilst not spending the time talking with compatriots in their native language. Others do not guarantee that this will be the case, but do say that a guest will not be asked to share a room with someone of the same nationality. It is wise to clarify the situation well in advance with the organisation in question. Some stays offer the option of half or full board, and sometimes bed and breakfast, but the majority of stays, particularly those for the younger age groups, include full board. Any special dietary needs should be stated on the application form. Do remember

that you are being welcomed into somebody's home, and that you should respect it accordingly. It may not have the same facilities as your own, and a certain amount of tolerance and goodwill will be needed on both sides.

Escorted travel Many organisations either include travel in their basic fee or are able to offer assistance with making arrangements. In some cases such services are available only at extra cost, and this is always indicated in the entry. Often organised travel is in escorted groups, and this is a particularly good idea for young people not used to travelling alone. Most organisations will arrange for host families to meet their guests at a central meeting point, either at the airport, port or the local station. If you are making your own arrangements you should contact your host family to decide on a meeting point and to check whether they will be able to help with travel to the departure point for the return journey. Practical Information has further advice.

Insurance Insurance cover is not always included in the price of the stay, but is often available at extra cost. Make sure that you know exactly what cover you will receive as some policies provide only basic cover. See Practical Information for further advice.

Other services Details of other areas of the organisation's related activities are included here, for example penfriend services and other exchange opportunities.

Additional information Any further details of relevance to the stay, for example where a welfare service is available, where early application is essential and if any references or particular attributes are required, are included here.

Handicapped participants Certain
organisations are able to arrange
stays for handicapped people, and
these are indicated by **H** . When
applying state the exact nature of
the disability and any special care
or facilities required. Even if **H** is
not indicated in an entry it is worth
making enquiries if you feel that the
handicap is not likely to put
unreasonable demands on the
organiser or the host family.

FIYTO indicates a member of the
Federation of International Youth
Travel Organisations, a worldwide
federation of organisations
specialising in youth travel. FIYTO
aims to promote educational,
cultural and social travel among
young people.

FIOCES indicates a member of the
Federation Internationale des
Organisations de Correspondences
et d'Echanges Scolaires, founded in
1929 to help bring together young
people of all nations by furthering
international school exchanges.
Member organisations must
provide sufficient moral,
pedagogical and technical
guarantees, and work in agreement
with education authorities.

HOMESTAYS
MAINLAND EUROPE

FRANCE

Organisation ACTE International

Address 6 avenue Maurice Ravel, 75012 Paris, France Tel 43 42 48 84

Profile A non-profitmaking organisation founded in 1976 promoting, in collaboration with the French education authorities, educational and cultural travel for young people

Areas Paris area

Ages 18-30

Stay 2/3 weeks, all year

Level of language required Basic knowledge of French

Language tuition Homestays with French language programmes in Brittany, July/August

Activities Host families organise visits to local places of interest

Accommodation Single/twin bedrooms

Costs FF2160 2 weeks, FF2980 3 weeks, full board

Escorted travel Not provided

Insurance Not provided

Other services Study and discovery tours, tailored programmes, language courses and 1 year university programmes

FIYTO

FRANCE, FEDERAL REPUBLIC OF GERMANY, GREECE

Organisation Anglia International En Famille Homestay Agency

Address 154 Fronks Road, Dovercourt, Harwich, Essex CO12 4EF Tel Harwich 503717

Profile A private commercial organisation founded in 1983, arranging homestays for young people and adults

Areas France: mainly Provence and the south

Germany: mainly in the west

Greece: mainly Athens

Ages 10+

Stay Weekly, all year

Language tuition English study courses arranged for groups

Accommodation Host families provide personal references which are taken up, and great importance is placed on these. Families and guests are matched according to interests and hobbies.

Costs £82 per week full board; agency fee £19

Escorted travel Can be provided

Insurance Arranged on request

FRANCE

Organisation Aquitaine Service Linguistique

Address 15 Allee des Genets, Domaine de Terre-Rouge, 33127 Martignas, France Tel 56 21 40 96

Profile A non-profitmaking organisation founded in 1978 arranging homestays, exchange visits and language courses

Areas Bordeaux, Cognac, Pays Basque, Perigord, Charentes areas

Ages 12+

Stay 1+ weeks, all year

Level of language required All levels of French accepted

Language tuition French courses available in Bordeaux

Activities Families arrange outings; cultural/sports facilities available in most areas

Accommodation Single/shared bedrooms in carefully selected families of similar backgrounds and interests, with children of same age where appropriate.

Costs From FF900 half board, FF1050 full board, per week; registration fee FF180

Escorted travel Participants are normally met at the airport/station by the family

Insurance Not provided

Other services Exchange visits, au pair placements and language courses

UK representation Baxter's Agency & School of English, PO Box 12, Peterborough, Cambridgeshire PE3 6JN Tel Peterborough 62744/53463

FRANCE

Organisation Association pour les Voyages Educatifs (AVE)/ Maison de Cambridge

Address 1 rue General Riu, 34000 Montpellier, France Tel 67 64 07 86

Profile A non-profitmaking voluntary organisation. AVE is an educational visit/exchange organisation founded in 1984; Maison de Cambridge, founded in 1978 as the Centre Britanique, is a British cultural centre set up in 1985 by members of the local education authorities in Montpellier and Cambridge as part of Community Link.

Areas Montpellier, Nimes, Beziers, Sete, Aix-en-Provence

Ages 13-20

Stay 2+ weeks

Level of language required Elementary

Language tuition Not provided

Activities Hosts treat visitors as members of the family and often arrange outings

Accommodation Particular attention is paid to compatibility of host family and guest. Families are chosen for their willingness to participate in activities with visitors, and have children of the same age as the guest. Single bedrooms.

Costs On request; FF60 annual subscription

Escorted travel Groups of 5-10 children travel together, escorted by one teacher

Insurance Holiday risk/cancellation insurance provided

UK representation Community Education Department, Shire Hall, Cambridge/Montpellier Exchange Register, Rainey Endowed School, Magherafelt, Northern Ireland

Other services Exchanges and schooling abroad, au pair placements and working holidays

Additional information To ensure that visiting children do not speak too much of their own language no courses or activities are arranged after the initial group travel

EUROPE

Organisation Baxter's Agency & School of English

Address PO Box 12, Peterborough, Cambridgeshire PE3 6JN Tel Peterborough 62744/53463

Profile A private organisation founded in 1963, encouraging young people to visit areas abroad not commonly visited by tourists and to become involved in the family and social life of the country

Areas Austria: all areas

Belgium: French-speaking areas

France: south

Germany: mostly Bavaria

Spain: mostly Barcelona and surrounding area

Ages 15-25

Stay 2-4 weeks, all year

Level of language required Depends on area visited

Language tuition Language courses on request

Activities Sports and activities

Accommodation In friendly families, some of whom may have young people of the same age as the guests

Costs From £50 half board, £70 full board, per week. Registration fee £10/£15.

Escorted travel Not provided

Insurance Provided

Other services Au pair placements

FRANCE

Organisation The Central Bureau

Address 16 Malone Road, Belfast BT9 5BN Tel 0232-664418/9

Profile The Central Bureau was established in 1948 by the British government to act as the national information office and coordinating unit for every type of educational visit and exchange. The Northern Ireland office opened in 1980.

Areas Angouleme, Poitiers

Ages 14-19

Stay 3 weeks, July and August

Level of language required Basic knowledge of French

Language tuition None provided

Activities Host families may arrange outings

Accommodation In families carefully selected by Visites et Echanges Culturels et Sportifs Internationaux. The emphasis is on experiencing life; there is no guarantee that there will be a young person of the same age in the family.

Costs £310, 3 weeks, inclusive of travel

Escorted travel Accompanied coach travel provided

Insurance Provided

Other services Home to home exchanges, term time stays in German schools, English language camps, junior assistantships, school and class links, teacher exchanges, in-service training courses, and study and hospitality visits

Additional information Northern Ireland applicants only

H depending on availability

FRANCE

Organisation The Central Bureau

Address 3 Bruntsfield Crescent, Edinburgh EH10 4HD Tel 031-447 8024

Profile The Central Bureau was established in 1948 by the British government to act as the national information office and coordinating unit for every type of educational visit and exchange. The Scottish office opened in 1972.

Areas Poitou-Charentes region

Ages 14-18

Stay 3 weeks, July and August

Level of language required 2 years French

Language tuition None provided

Activities Family outings

Accommodation In families carefully selected by Visites et Echanges Culturels et Sportifs Internationaux. The emphasis is on experiencing life; there is no guarantee that there will be a young person of the same age in the family.

Costs £305, 3 weeks, includes full board, travel and insurance

Escorted travel By coach from Edinburgh

Insurance Provided

Other services Home to home exchanges, term time stays in German schools, English language camps, junior assistantships, school and class links, teacher exchanges, in-service training courses, and study and hospitality visits

Additional information Scottish applicants only

H accepted

SPAIN

Organisation Centros Europeos

Address Calle Principe, 12-6o A-28012, Madrid, Spain Tel 232 72 30

Profile A private company founded in 1968 aiming to give young people the opportunity of discovering a foreign culture and improving their knowledge of languages through homestays and exchanges

Areas Madrid, Valencia, Alicante, Segovia and small towns along the Mediterranean coast

Ages 10+

Stay 1-4+ weeks, Easter and summer

Level of language required Basic knowledge of Spanish

Language tuition Stays can be combined with language courses in Madrid, Valencia, and Alicante

Activities Local visits and excursions organised; some families arrange outings

Accommodation Half/full board accommodation with carefully selected families; single or shared bedrooms

Costs From Pts 12,500 per week, half board; reductions for groups

Escorted travel Guests can be met at airport/station at extra cost

Insurance Public liability insurance provided

Other services Language programmes, exchange visits and au pair placements

Additional information A representative of the organisation is always on hand to deal with any problems

H

FRANCE

Organisation Club des 4 Vents

Address 1 rue Gozlin, 75006 Paris, France Tel 43 29 60 20

Profile A non-profitmaking organisation founded in 1953, specialising in international meetings and exchanges for young people wishing to improve their knowledge of a foreign language and discover other ways of life

Areas Paris area (except July/August), Cognac region, Amiens, Sete and Lyon; farmstays in Amiens and Agen areas

Ages 12-20, depending on area

Stay 2/3 weeks, all year

Level of language required 2/3 years knowledge of French for stays without courses

Language tuition French courses available

Activities Meetings, sports and excursions

Accommodation Families are carefully chosen by local coordinators for their warmth and hospitality

Costs From FF1940 2 weeks, full board; half board in Paris only from FF1980. Farmstays from FF2880 3 weeks.

Escorted travel Host families meet students at stations/airports

Insurance Not provided

Other services Study tours, programmes for sports teams/music groups, and international centre for seminars and conferences

FIYTO

EUROPE

Organisation Contacts In Britain

Address PO Box 10, Rye, East Sussex TN31 6BW Tel Rye 882444

Profile A commercial organisation founded in 1970, arranging linguistic and sightseeing stays in Europe

Areas France: all areas, particularly Brittany, Normandy, the Loire Valley, Dordogne, Bordeaux and Grenoble

Denmark, Germany and Spain: limited areas

Ages 10-60

Stay 1+ weeks, all year

Language tuition Can be arranged

Accommodation Families are carefully chosen for their suitability in receiving foreign visitors; every effort is made to match visitors with families having similar interests and backgrounds

Costs France: FF1790 1 week, full board; FF1200 for each subsequent week. Half board arrangements can be made. £50 registration/administration fee.

Denmark, Germany and Spain: costs on application

Escorted travel Not provided

Insurance Not provided

Other services Language courses, sports visits, specially prepared programmes for groups or individuals, linguistic and discovery homestay programmes for groups, and au pair placements

H given sufficient notice

FEDERAL REPUBLIC OF GERMANY

Organisation Deutsch In Deutschland GmbH

Address Hauptstrasse 26, 8751 Stockstadt/Main, Federal Republic of Germany Tel 6027/1251

Profile A non-profitmaking organisation founded in 1980, arranging a wide variety of German language courses and homestays

Areas All over the Federal Republic; combined homestay and sports/leisure programme arranged at centres in Ascheffenburg, Bad Krenznach, Bamberg, Hanau, Mannheim, Nurnberg, Oldenburg, Schwabach and Siegen

Ages 10+

Stay 2/3 weeks, all year

Level of language required Minimum 1 years knowledge for courses; beginners accepted on request

Language tuition Arrange tuition which can be combined with sports courses

Activities Excursions, sports

Accommodation All families are very carefully selected; wherever possible host families have children of the same age as the guest

Costs DM700 2 weeks, DM1000 3 weeks, DM305 for each extra week, full board. Bed and breakfast and half board also available. DM805 2 weeks, DM1145 3 weeks for combined homestay and sports/leisure programme.

Escorted travel Can be arranged from airport to centre at extra cost

Insurance Arranged on request

H on request

FRANCE, FEDERAL REPUBLIC OF GERMANY

Organisation Dragons International

Address The Old Vicarage, South Newington, Banbury, Oxfordshire OX15 4JN Tel Banbury 721717

Profile A commercial organisation founded in 1975, enabling young people to spend 2/3 weeks living as a member of a family abroad on a homestay or exchange basis

Areas Throughout France and the Federal Republic of Germany

Ages 11-19

Stay 2/3 weeks, March-April, July-August

Level of language required Basic knowledge

Language tuition None provided

Activities Host families arrange outings

Accommodation Single/shared rooms in carefully selected families having young people of similar age or background

Costs £75 per week full board

Escorted travel Fully supervised coach transport from 13 points in the UK to 12 points in France and Germany from £99

Insurance Provided

Other services Exchange visits

FIOCES

FRANCE

Organisation Echanges Culturels Internationaux

Address 62 avenue Delattre de Tassigny, 13100 Aix-en-Provence, France Tel 21 07 68

Profile A non-profitmaking organisation founded in 1975, arranging homestays with French families

Areas Provence, Cote d'Azur

Ages 14-30

Stay 1-4 weeks

Level of language required 2 years knowledge of French

Language tuition Arranged for groups on request

Activities Family outings; excursions can be arranged for groups

Accommodation Families are chosen with great care by local organisers; where possible hosts will have children of the same age

Costs FF1050 per week full board; half board also available

Escorted travel Guests are met at rail stations and transferred to the host family; extra charge for airport transfers

Insurance Public liability insurance provided

Other services Tailor-made tours for groups

EUROPE

Organisation En Famille Agency (Overseas)

Address Westbury House, Queens Lane, Arundel, Sussex BN18 9JN
Tel Arundel 883266

Profile A private company founded in 1945 offering holidays for
travellers wishing to learn or practise a foreign language in private
family homes abroad

Areas Throughout Austria, Belgium, France, Federal Republic of
Germany, Italy, Portugal, Spain and Switzerland

Ages 12-90

Stay Weekly, all year

Level of language required About 2 years study

Language tuition French courses can be arranged in Paris, La
Rochelle and Tours; optional teaching facilities for school groups

Activities Guests take part in family outings

Accommodation Host families are all personally inspected. Particular
care is taken to match the family with the individual's requirements,
details of background, interests and facilities being carefully compared.

Costs £60-£92 half board, £85-£105 full board, per week. Registration
fee £12; selection and booking fee £18.

Escorted travel Arranged on request. Host families can meet visitors
at airports/station at extra cost.

Insurance Provided

Other services In France: teenage group holidays with language
courses, stays for a term or a year, independent language holidays

Additional information Participants must provide two references. The
choice of areas/families in Italy, Austria, Switzerland, Portugal and
Belgium will be more limited than in France, Germany and Spain.

FRANCE, FEDERAL REPUBLIC OF GERMANY, SPAIN

Organisation Euro Academy Ltd

Address 77a George Street, Croydon, Surrey CR0 1LD Tel 01-681 2905

Profile A private organisation founded in 1971 to develop the relationships between young people throughout the world by bringing them together on both study and activity courses/visits

Areas France: Paris, Amiens, Aix-en-Provence, Cote d'Azur, Toulon, Avignon, Clermont-Ferrand, Lyon, Montpellier, Sete and Cognac

Germany: Ascheffenburg, Wurzburg, Wiesbaden, Nurnberg, Augsburg, Cologne, Hannover and Mannheim

Spain: Zamora, Valladolid, Madrid and Valencia

Ages France: 12+ Germany: 10-21 Spain: 14-26

Stay France: 1/2+ weeks, all year except July/August (Paris and Cote d'Azur). Germany and Spain: 2+ weeks, (Valencia 1+weeks), all year.

Level of language required Knowledge not necessary but helpful

Language tuition Organise vacation courses which can be combined with family accommodation

Activities Families may arrange outings

Accommodation Families are selected for their hospitality; single/twin bedrooms

Costs France: £115 6 nights, £206 13 nights, full board; half board in Paris. Germany: £200 2 weeks, £285 3 weeks, £375 4 weeks, full board. Spain: From £102 full board, 2 weeks; £67 half board, per week (Valencia only)

Escorted travel On arrival at station on request

Insurance Not provided

Other services Vacation and university courses, and educational tours

FIYTO

FRANCE, FEDERAL REPUBLIC OF GERMANY

Organisation Eurolanguage Ltd

Address Greyhound House, 23/24 George Street, Richmond, Surrey TW9 1HY Tel 01-940 1087/948 5846

Profile A commercial organisation founded in 1972, concerned with the promotion of the life, culture and language of France and Germany

Areas France: Paris, Nice, Le Touquet

Germany: Kiel

Ages 11-18

Stay 2 weeks, all year

Level of language required No knowledge necessary

Language tuition Study courses available

Activities Family outings; excursions for groups

Accommodation Single bedrooms in selected host families, who are all interviewed personally; close contact is maintained with them at all times. They are selected to match the needs, interests and background of each guest.

Costs £114 per week full board + £100 per additional week

Escorted travel Guests can be met at airports/ports; escorted travel for groups

Insurance Provided

Other services Mini holidays and day trips

Additional information 24 hour back-up service

H subject to available and suitable families

FEDERAL REPUBLIC OF GERMANY

Organisation Europa-Sprachclub GmbH

Address Bismarckstrasse 89, 4000 Dusseldorf Tel 36 43 78 or Stuttgarterstrasse 161, 7014 Kornwestheim, Federal Republic of Germany Tel 60 28

Profile A commercial organisation founded in 1959 offering a wide range of linguistic holidays for young people and adults

Areas Dusseldorf, Stuttgart and small towns in the south: Freiburg in Breisgau, Black Forest, Tubingen

Ages 15+

Stay 2+ weeks, all year

Level of language required 1 years knowledge of German

Language tuition German courses arranged at centres which can be combined with homestays

Activities Excursion and activity programmes.

Accommodation Carefully selected families, which are individually visited and evaluated; single/twin bedrooms

Costs DM860 2 weeks full board; DM320 for each additional week. DM 1840 6 weeks and DM2280 8 weeks.

Escorted travel Participants can be met by the host family

Insurance Third party liability insurance provided

Other services Holiday, intensive, professional and family language courses

FIYTO

FRANCE, FEDERAL REPUBLIC OF GERMANY

Organisation European Educational Opportunities Programme

Address 28 Canterbury Road, Lydden, Dover, Kent CT15 7ER Tel Dover 823631

Profile A non-profitmaking organisation founded in 1986 aiming to offer high-quality programmes through carefully selected homes, schools and allied agencies

Areas France: Paris and Auxerre

Germany: Dusseldorf and Munich

Ages 10+

Stay 2+ weeks, all year

Level of language required Basic knowledge desirable

Language tuition Language courses can be arranged

Activities Excursions arranged

Accommodation Students are totally integrated into the family

Costs From £55 per week, full board

Escorted travel Participants are met at port of arrival

Insurance Not provided

Other services Residential term stays at independent boarding schools, city adventure and work experience programmes, class visits, programmes for adults and professional study tours

Overseas representation France: ANEAS, 54 Grande Rue, 89113 Fleury la Vallee

Federal Republic of Germany: Jeuneurope-Studienfahrten, Oststrasse 162, 4000 Dusseldorf 1

EUROPE

Organisation Euroyouth Ltd

Address 301 Westborough Road, Westcliff-on-Sea, Essex SS0 9PT Tel 0702 341434

Profile A commercial organisation founded in 1961 with the aim of offering facilities for young people to practise the language which they are learning in a family setting

Areas Austria: Vienna and various towns in the provinces

Belgium: Brussels and French, Dutch or German-speaking families in various areas

France: Paris, Tours, Cannes, Nice, Antibes, Menton and small villages along the Cote d'Azur, Aix-en-Provence, Clermont-Ferrand, Les Sables d'Olonne

Germany: Cologne, Munich, Dusseldorf, Stuttgart and Wurzburg

Greece: Athens   Italy: Genoa, Florence, Naples, Perugia

Netherlands: all areas   Portugal: Lisbon

Spain: Barcelona   Turkey: Istanbul and Ankara

Ages 17+

Stay 2+ weeks, all year

Level of language required Basic knowledge useful

Language tuition Courses available in Austria, France, Germany, Italy, Portugal and Spain

Activities Sports activities available; family outings at extra cost

Accommodation In selected and inspected private homes

Costs £80-£120 per week, depending on country and terms; bed and breakfast, half and full board available. Registration placement fee £43.

Escorted travel Arranged on request at extra cost

Insurance Obligatory insurance provided

Other services Study and sports courses, educational seminars

Additional information Welfare service available, advice and assistance provided during stay. Apply 4-6 weeks in advance.

H limited opportunities

FIYTO FIOCES

EUROPE

Organisation Euroyouth Ltd

Address 301 Westborough Road, Westcliff-on-Sea, Essex SS0 9PT Tel 0702 341434

Profile A commercial organisation founded in 1961 with the aim of offering facilities for young people to practise the language which they are learning in a family setting and to experience the way of life of the country they are visiting

Areas Throughout Austria, Greece, Italy, Portugal and Spain; limited opportunities in Belgium, France and Germany

Ages 15-25

Stay 2/3 weeks, all year

Level of language required Basic knowledge useful

Language tuition Language courses available

Activities Opportuntiies for visits, cultural activities and sports

Accommodation Under this arrangement applicants live as guests with a family in return for undertaking several hours daily English conversation with the children or hosts. There is also time for the guest to practise their knowledge of the native language. Single/twin bedrooms.

Costs Registration fee £3; placement fee £45. Accommodation and food provided under en famille conditions.

Escorted travel Arranged on request at extra cost

Insurance Obligatory insurance provided

Additional information Applicants mother tongue must be English; early application essential. Welfare service available, advice and assistance provided during stay if required.

H limited opportunities

FIYTO FIOCES

EUROPE

Organisation The Experiment in International Living

Address Otesaga, West Malvern Road, Upper Wyche, Malvern, Worcestershire WR14 4EN Tel Malvern 62577

Profile A non-profitmaking educational travel organisation founded in 1936 with the aim of promoting understanding, friendship and respect between people from different cultural backgrounds

Areas Throughout Belgium, Czechoslovakia, Denmark, France, Federal Republic of Germany, Greece, Italy, Netherlands, Poland, Portugal, Spain and Switzerland

Ages 16+

Stay 1-4 weeks, all year

Level of language required None necessary

Language tuition Courses can be arranged

Activities Families usually arrange outings. Activities and excursions included in group programmes. Professional courses, eg farming, social work, can be arranged on request

Accommodation Varies from single room to floor space, depending on family. Families are carefully selected with the understanding that the aim is to allow individuals to experience a different way of life; the circumstances and beliefs of the host family may therefore differ from those of the participants.

Costs From £109-£143 per week full board, depending on country; travel extra. Occasional grant aid available on some programmes.

Escorted travel Group travel arrangements made; arrangements for individuals on request. Host families will meet participants at airport/station if requested.

Insurance Provided

Other services Special interest programmes

Overseas representation Over 45 offices worldwide: details from UK office

Additional information Apply 8-10 weeks in advance

FRANCE, FEDERAL REPUBLIC OF GERMANY

Organisation Gesellschaft fur Internationale Jugendkontakte eV

Address Am Helpert 32-34, Postfach 200 562, 5300 Bonn 2, Federal Republic of Germany Tel 32 26 49

Profile A non-profitmaking organisation founded in 1983, arranging homestays and exchanges

Areas France: Tours, Dinan, Caen, Montpellier, St Brieuc, La Ciotat, Aix-en-Provence, Sete, Grenoble

Federal Republic of Germany: Bamberg, Wurzburg, Hannover, Fulda, Kassel

Ages 10-21

Stay 1-4 weeks, Easter and summer

Level of language required Fair knowledge preferable

Language tuition Optional language courses can be arranged

Activities Excursions arranged with language courses

Accommodation All families are visited and carefully selected, and are matched with guests according to background, hobbies, interests and location

Costs From DM350 per week

Escorted travel Can be arranged

Insurance Can be arranged

Other services Exchanges, summer schools and courses, au pair placements and guides on work and study opportunities for young people

FRANCE, FEDERAL REPUBLIC OF GERMANY, SPAIN

Organisation Host & Guest Service

Address 592A King's Road, London SW6 2DX Tel 01-731 5340

Profile A private organisation founded in 1956, providing a wide variety of reliable accommodation with families according to individual needs

Areas France: most areas, especially Brittany, Normandy, Tours and Paris

Germany: Munich

Spain: Barcelona and San Sebastian

Ages All ages; young children will need to be accompanied by an adult

Stay To suit individual requirements

Language tuition Details of local language schools provided on request

Activities Families may arrange outings

Accommodation Offer an individual service, ensuring compatibility of host and guest; young people are placed in homes with young people of similar interests

Costs £65-£120 full board, £60-£90 half board, £40-£75 bed and breakfast, per week. Service charge £30.

Escorted travel Adults are met at local stations; young people can be met at airport/station at occasional extra cost

Insurance Arranged on request

Other services Au pair placements

H placed where possible

AUSTRIA, FEDERAL REPUBLIC OF GERMANY, SWITZERLAND

Organisation International Catholic Service for Homestays and Penfriends

Address Veilchenweg 2, 6634 Wallerfangen, Federal Republic of Germany Tel 60638

Profile A voluntary non-profitmaking organisation founded in 1950, offering a paying guest service

Areas Towns and villages in Austria, Germany and Switzerland

Ages 12-25

Stay 2-4 weeks, Christmas/Easter holidays, and 15 June-30 September

Level of language required Minimum 2 years study

Language tuition Not provided

Accommodation In selected friendly, hospitable and Christian families

Costs DM300-DM1070 depending on facilities and length of stay; registration fee DM70

Escorted travel Not provided

Insurance Included

Other services Penfriend service

Additional information Character references required; applicants must be students or undertaking vocational training. Apply at least 4 weeks in advance.

FRANCE

Organisation Inter Sejours

Address 4 rue de Parme, 75009 Paris, France Tel 42 80 09 38 and 179 rue de Courcelles, 75017 Paris, France Tel 47 63 06 81

Profile A non-profitmaking organisation founded in 1968, arranging homestays, linguistic stays and au pair placements

Areas Paris, Vallee de la Loire

Ages 12-18

Stay 2+ weeks, all year

Language tuition Combined homestay/language course available

Activities Outings arranged by families

Accommodation Information about the host family is sent to the participant in advance, so that correspondence can take place beforehand if desired. Single or shared bedrooms.

Costs From FF2500 (provinces), FF3100 (Paris), 2 weeks full board. Registration fee FF150.

Escorted travel Participants are met at the nearest station; transfers from Paris on request

Insurance Provided

Other services Combined homestay/language/activity holidays and au pair placements

Additional information Apply at least 2 months in advance

FRANCE, FEDERAL REPUBLIC OF GERMANY

Organisation Interspeak Ltd

Address 14 Robin Hill Drive, Standish, near Wigan, Greater Manchester WN6 0QW Tel Standish 421960

Profile A commercial organisation founded in 1981 to provide good family accommodation for foreign students and to improve international relationships among young people

Areas France: Paris, Angouleme

Germany: Munich

Ages 12+

Stay April-October, individuals; April-August, groups

Language tuition Language holidays arranged in France; courses may be available in Germany

Activities Families outings; organised activities available as part of language course

Accommodation Single bedroom in family with teenage children where possible

Costs France: from £150 per week, full board (Paris), £138 (Angouleme, full board with tuition). Germany: £150 per week, full board.

Escorted travel Travel can be arranged

Insurance Provided

Other services Exchange visits, language holidays and French cookery courses

Overseas representation VECSI, 10 rue Ludovic Trarieux, 16007 Angouleme, France Tel 95 73 57

H accepted

FRANCE

Organisation La Ligue d'Amitie Internationale

Address 54 boulevard de Vaugirard, 75015 Paris, France Tel 43 20 96 29

Profile A non-profit making voluntary organisation founded in 1931 with the aim of increasing international understanding among young people

Areas Paris and Nantes

Ages 14+

Stay 1+ weeks

Level of language required Basic French helpful

Language tuition Can be arranged at extra cost

Activities Excursions arranged as part of some stays

Accommodation Single/twin bedrooms in member families of the Ligue

Costs FF815 half board, FF1115 full board. FF60 booking fee, FF45 membership fee.

Escorted travel Individuals met at local station by host family

Insurance Provided

Other services Exchanges, study stays at international holidays centres, craft holidays, workcamps and international penfriend scheme

FIOCES

FRANCE

Organisation Morrissey Linguistic Centre Ltd

Address Valhall, Killinure, Athlone, Co Westmeath, Ireland Tel Athlone 85160

Profile A commercial organisation founded in 1969 organising language courses, homestays, farmstays and riding programmes

Areas Throughout France

Ages 12-18

Stay 3 weeks

Level of language required 1 years knowledge of French

Language tuition None provided

Activities Excursions arranged

Accommodation In private family homes

Costs £365 full board, inclusive of return travel from Dublin

Escorted travel Escorted travel with overnight stays and transfers where necessary provided

Insurance Provided

EUROPE

Organisation Naturfreundejugend Deutschlands

Address Intercultur, Rosenstrasse 1, 4806 Werther, Federal Republic of Germany Tel (0) 5203-5109/5204-5711

Profile A voluntary non-profitmaking organisation founded in 1895 to offer cultural experience and political education to working people. It provides a service in particular for the less well-off and the socially disadvantaged.

Areas Throughout Germany, Italy, Netherlands, Spain and Switzerland

Ages No limits

Stay 1-3 weeks, all year

Level of language required None necessary

Language tuition None provided

Activities Host families are not obliged to arrange anything but careful matching ensures that host and guest share similar interests

Accommodation Varies from single room to floor space, depending on family. Hosts and guests are matched carefully with particular attention given to knowledge of languages. Meals provided by mutual arrangement.

Costs Hosts and guests arrange contribution to household expenses, approx £20-£25 per week. Agency fee £20.

Escorted travel Not provided

Insurance Not provided

Overseas representation UK: Mrs S Kortlandt, Intercultur, 91 Marlborough Gardens, Upminster, Essex RM14 1SQ Tel Upminster 25617

Italy: Elena Rossi, Via Trieste 11/A, 1-20081 Abbiategrasso (MI) Tel 02/9467657

Netherlands: Ted Beets, Nivon Jeugd & Jongeren, PC Hooftstraat 163, 1071 BV Amsterdam Tel 020-626003

H

MALTA

Organisation NSTS Student and Youth Travel

Address 220 St Paul Street, Valletta, Malta Tel 624983/626628

Aims A non-profitmaking organisation founded in 1955 to provide young people with the opportunity of widening their knowledge and education through travel, contacts and exchanges

Areas Residential areas of Sliema and suburbs

Ages 12-30

Stay 1 week-3 months, all year; ages 30+ September-June only

Language tuition English courses arranged

Activities In addition to those arranged by the host family, day excursions, leisure activities and sports are organised on request in winter and regularly, June-September

Accommodation Single/twin bedrooms

Costs M£30 per week full board, including one cultural activity/excursion

Escorted travel Free escort provided for groups of 25+

Insurance Provided on request

Other services Arts, crafts and computer courses arranged all year

FIYTO

AUSTRIA

Organisation Osterreichisches Komitee fur Internationalen
Studienaustausch (OKISTA)

Address 1090 Vienna 9, Turkenstrasse 4, Austria Tel 347526

Profile A non-profitmaking organisation founded in 1950 by the
Austrian government, serving the youth and student community of
Austria as well as many individuals and groups from other countries

Areas Most cities in Austria

Ages 16-30

Stay 1+ weeks

Language tuition Arrange a wide range of German language courses

Costs AS150 bed & breakfast, AS200 half board, per day; registration
fee AS250

Escorted travel Not provided

Insurance Not provided

Other services German language courses, camps and international
youth holiday centres, au pair visits, sightseeing/study tours, and youth
travel and accommodation service

FIYTO

AUSTRIA

Organisation Osterreichische Vereinigung fur Austausch und Studienreisen (OVAST)

Address Dr Gschmeidlerstrasse 10/4, 3500 Krems, PO Box 148, Austria Tel 02732 5743

Profile A non-profitmaking organisation founded in 1964 arranging homestays and exchanges

Areas Austria

Ages mainly 10-20

Stay 1-52 weeks, all year

Language tuition German lessons arranged at extra cost

Activities Outings and social activities arranged

Accommodation In selected families

Costs AS1580 per week full board plus AS300 enrolment fee

Escorted travel By train/bus/air provided

Insurance Provided

Other services Skiing holidays

FIYTO FIOCES

FRANCE

Organisation PGL School Tours

Address Station Street, Ross-on-Wye, Herefordshire HR9 7AH Tel Ross-on-Wye 64211

Profile A commercial organisation founded in 1957, offering a wide range of tailor-made educational holidays and tours for groups

Areas Paris suburbs, Loire Valley and Le Havre

Ages 11+

Stay 4+ days, all year

Level of language required Rudimentary understanding of French

Activities Complete programme of excursions organised

Accommodation All accommodation is carefully inspected by local organisers. Families are chosed for their readiness to accommodate English schoolchildren, and wherever possible participants are placed with families who have children of a similar age. Single/twin bedrooms.

Costs From £102 4 days Le Havre, £144 8 days Loire Valley, £151 1 week Paris, full board, per person

Escorted travel Return coach/ferry travel from school or college to destination provided

Insurance Included

Other services PGL Young Adventure arrange activity and sports holidays for individuals, groups and families

H Suitable families selected on receipt of full details

FEDERAL REPUBLIC OF GERMANY

Organisation Reisezirkel-Jeuneurope

Address Oststrasse 162, 4000 Dusseldorf 1, Federal Republic of Germany Tel 35 28 26

Profile A commercial organisation founded in 1954, arranging homestays, family holidays, language courses, and school visits for German children and adults

Areas Dusseldorf, Siegburg

Ages 12+

Stay 2+ weeks

Level of language required Basic knowledge

Language tuition Can be arranged

Activities Outings with host family

Accommodation Single bedrooms, occasionally shared

Costs From DM350 per week full board; half board also available

Escorted travel Host families meet guests at airport/station

Insurance Not provided

Other services Riding holidays

FRANCE

Organisation The Robertson Organisation

Address 44 Willoughby Road, London NW3 1RU Tel 01-435 4907

Profile A private organisation founded in 1948 to promote language learning and understanding among young people of Europe

Areas Paris area

Ages 11-21

Stay 2-3 weeks Easter and July/August

Language tuition 4 mornings per week

Activities Excursions to Paris and Versailles

Accommodation Single/twin bedrooms in carefully selected families, usually with children of the same age/sex

Costs From £330-£415 2/3 weeks full board, inclusive of travel, excursions and tuition

Escorted travel In escorted groups ex London by train and boat

Insurance Can be arranged

Other services Arrange exchange visits

Overseas representation L'Organisation Robertson, 51 rue de la Harpe, 75005 Paris, France Tel 46 33 12 89

Additional information Prefer to meet applicants and parents; appointments can be booked

H depending on nature of handicap

FIOCES

FRANCE

Organisation Sejours Internationaux Linguistiques et Culturels (SILC)

Address 32 Rempart de l'Est, 16022 Angouleme Cedex, France Tel 45 95 83 56

Profile A non-profitmaking organisation founded in 1965, aiming to develop skills in the educational field whilst favouring greater cultural interchange

Areas Paris region, Orleans, Limousin, Le Havre, Biarritz, Montpellier, Perpignan, Royan, Grenoble, Cote d'Azur, Bordeaux and Angouleme

Ages All ages

Stay 2+ weeks, all year, but mostly Christmas, Easter and summer vacations

Level of language required Basic knowledge of French necessary

Language tuition Personalised courses for groups on request

Activities Stays can be combined with an Entente Cordiale week of activities with young French people; group excursions and visits arranged on request

Accommodation Local organisers select host families and match them with participants; single/double bedrooms

Costs FF1235-FF1574 per week full board, depending on location; FF1000 registration fee

Escorted travel Can be arranged; participants can be met at stations/ports

Insurance Provided

Other services Cultural/sightseeing tours, study tours, in-service training courses and au pair placements

UK representation Mrs F Forrest-Evans, 50 Cypress Avenue, Whitton, Middlesex TW2 7JZ Tel 01-894 1151

H but no wheelchairs

FIYTO FIOCES

FRANCE, FEDERAL REPUBLIC OF GERMANY, SPAIN

Organisation Youth Travels Abroad

Address 117 Wendell Road, London W12 9SD Tel 01-743 7966

Profile A private organisation founded in 1961, arranging individual travel abroad to improve foreign language ability

Areas France: Tours, Grenoble, La Rochelle, Nimes, Montpellier, St-Brieuc, Caen, Chambery, Dax, Lucon, Flers, Pau, Bourges, Laval, Nantes, Dinard, Vannes, Val de Loire and Nice

Germany: Dusseldorf, Stuttgart, Tubingen, Freiburg and other smaller towns in the south

Spain: Valencia

Ages France: 14+; Germany: 15+; Spain: 16+

Stay France: 1/2+ weeks, all year except July and August. Germany: 2+ weeks, all year. Spain: weekly, all year.

Language tuition France: language courses can be combined with homestays in the Loire valley and the south. Germany and Spain: language courses can be combined with homestays.

Activities Sports and cultural activities available on courses

Accommodation Host families are carefully selected; single/twin bedrooms

Costs France: from £141 per week, £88 per additional week, full board

Germany: from £256 2 weeks, £94 per additional week, full board; £530 6 weeks, £665 8 weeks

Spain: £60 half board, £80 full board, per week; registration fee £20

Escorted travel Not available

Insurance Provided for France; on request for Germany and Spain

Additional information Group homestays in France only

HOMESTAYS

BRITAIN & IRELAND

ENGLAND

Organisation Academic Travel (Lowestoft) Ltd

Address The Briar School of English, 8 Gunton Cliff, Lowestoft, Suffolk NR32 4PE Tel Lowestoft 3781

Profile A commercial organisation founded in 1958, aiming to promote contact and travel among overseas people by assisting them to experience and enjoy the English way of life

Areas Lowestoft, Norwich, Great Yarmouth

Ages 18-70

Stay 2+ weeks, Easter and summer

Language tuition English courses available

Activities Sports, excursions, social programme; most families arrange outings

Accommodation Host families are visited and interviewed by accommodation and welfare officers to ensure that family and home meet set standards

Costs From £100 per week full board

Escorted travel Transfers by couriers from ports on certain days

Insurance Not provided

Other services English vacation courses for ages 10+ with optional sports tuition, and vacation courses for groups

Additional information 24 hour welfare service; immediate complaints/problems

IRELAND

Organisation Andrews Travel Consultants Ltd

Address 10 Meadow Vale, Blackrock, Co Dublin, Ireland Tel Dublin 894646/893930

Profile A private organisation founded in 1969 aiming to promote tourism in Ireland, organising a variety of holidays including private homestays

Areas Dublin, Bray, Galway, Cork, Limerick and Drogheda; other areas on request

Ages 12+

Stay Weekly, all year

Language tuition English courses arranged in Dublin and provincial centres

Activities Outings may be arranged by the host family

Accommodation Carefully selected families; single/twin bedrooms.

Costs IR£59 bed and breakfast, IR£72 half board, IR£88 full board, per week; ages 21+ £12-£14 per week extra

Escorted travel Not provided

Insurance Not provided

Other services Farmhouse, sports/activity and combined English language/activity holidays, summer camps and study courses

H on request

BRITAIN

Organisation Anglia International En Famille Homestay Agency

Address 154 Fronks Road, Dovercourt, Harwich, Essex CO12 4EF Tel Harwich 503717

Profile A private commercial organisation founded in 1983, arranging homestays for young people and adults

Areas Throughout Britain, especially in the east

Ages 10+

Stay Weekly, all year

Language tuition Tuition arranged for groups; also English study stays with private tutors

Accommodation Host families provide personal references which are taken up, and great importance is placed on these. Families and guests are matched according to interests and hobbies.

Costs £82 per week full board; agency fee £19

Escorted travel Can be provided

Insurance Arranged on request

ENGLAND

Organisation Anglo-German Contact

Address North Lodge, Colebrooke Park, Tonbridge, Kent TN11 0QD
Tel Tonbridge 823466

Profile A private organisation founded in 1982 aiming to help overseas
visitors improve their English by staying in friendly English families with
young people of the same age

Areas Tunbridge Wells and district

Ages 14-19/20

Stay Mid July-mid August

Level of English required 2 years study

Language tuition Optional private English tuition

Activities 3+ excursions per week; sports courses available at extra
cost

Accommodation Particular attention is paid to matching guests and
families according to hobbies and interests. Agency keeps in touch with
student and family throughout visit.

Costs £140 per week full board including excursions

Escorted travel Guests are met at airport/station as agreed with
parents

Insurance Not provided

Overseas representation Frau A Otto, Neuheikendorfer weg 23, 2305
Kiel-Heikendorf, Federal Republic of Germany

Additional information Apply before March

BRITAIN & IRELAND

Organisation Aquitaine Service Linguistique

Address 15 Allee des Genets, Domaine de Terre-Rouge, 33127 Martignas, France Tel 56 21 40 96

Profile A non-profitmaking organisation founded in 1978 arranging homestays, exchange visits and language courses

Areas South London, Brighton/Hove, Isle of Wight, Plymouth, Swansea, Canterbury and Oxford areas, the Midlands and Dublin

Ages Britain: 12+ depending on location; Ireland: 14+

Stay Britain: 1+ weeks, all year, except London (4+ days) and Oxford (2+ weeks); Ireland: 2+ weeks, all year

Level of English required All levels accepted

Language tuition Combined homestay/language courses available in most areas

Activities Cultural/sports facilities available in most areas

Accommodation Single/shared bedrooms in carefully selected families of similar backgrounds and interests, with children of same age where appropriate. Farmstays available in Ireland.

Costs Britain from FF880 4 days, FF1090 1 week, FF1980 2 weeks, half board; full board available in some areas at extra cost. Ireland from FF2280 2 weeks full board. Registration fee FF180.

Escorted travel Help given with travel arrangements; transfers included for stays in Plymouth and the Isle of Wight

Insurance Provided

Other services Language courses and au pair placements

ENGLAND

Organisation Association pour les Voyages Educatifs (AVE)/Maison de Cambridge

Address 1 rue General Riu, 34000 Montpellier, France Tel 67 64 07 86

Profile A non-profitmaking voluntary organisation. AVE is an educational visit/exchange organisation founded in 1984; Maison de Cambridge, founded in 1978 as the Centre Britanique, is a British cultural centre set up in 1985 by members of the local education authorities in Montpellier and Cambridge as part of Community Link.

Areas Usually Cambridge area

Ages 13-20

Stay 2+ weeks

Level of English required Elementary

Language tuition Not provided

Activities Hosts treat visitors as members of the family and often arrange outings

Accommodation Particular attention is paid to compatibility of host family and guest. Families are chosen for their willingness to participate in activities with visitors, and have children of the same age as the guest. Single bedrooms.

Costs £65-£80 per week full board plus travel; FF60 annual subscription

Escorted travel Groups of 5-10 children travel together, escorted by 1 teacher

Insurance Holiday risk/cancellation insurance provided

Other services Exchanges and schooling abroad, au pair placements and working holidays

Additional information To ensure that visiting children do not speak too much of their own language no courses or activities are arranged after the initial group travel

ENGLAND

Organisation Avalon Student Travel

Address 46 Withdean Road, Brighton, Sussex BN1 5BP Tel Brighton 553417

Profile A commercial organisation founded in 1963 with the aim of enabling young people have a low-cost holiday learning English in a family

Areas Brighton/Hove and surrounding area; villages and small towns in Sussex

Ages 15+ individuals; 12+ groups

Stay 1+ weeks, individuals; 3+ days, groups

Language tuition Can be arranged at associate study centre

Activities Families will sometimes arrange outings; excursion programme for groups

Accommodation All host families are visited and inspected. Students are sent a description and photograph of the family and details of the accommodation offered.

Costs £43.50-£67.50 half-board; £49.50 full board (suburbs only) per week. Single room supplement £2.50 per week. Reductions for groups.

Escorted travel Escort arrangements for individuals available at extra cost. Groups can be met on arrival at ports/airports with coach transport.

Insurance Arranged on request

Other services Holidays, language courses and accommodation

Additional information 24 hour emergency telephone service; accommodation secretary available to investigate any problems

ENGLAND

Organisation Baxter's Agency & School of English

Address PO Box 12, Peterborough, Cambridgeshire PE3 6JN Tel Peterborough 62744/53463

Profile A private organisation founded in 1963, encouraging young people to see areas of Britain not commonly visited by tourists and to become involved in English family and social life

Areas Cambridge, Peterborough, London and Brighton

Ages 14-25

Stay Weekly, all year

Language tuition English courses and private tuition arranged on request

Activities Excursions, sports and social and cultural activities

Accommodation In friendly families, some of whom may have young people of the same age

Costs From £45 half board, £50 full board, per week. Enrolment fee £10.

Escorted travel Escorts from most major ports/airports (except Gatwick) and stations can be arranged at extra cost

Insurance Provided

Other services Summer stays and language courses with full activity and social programmes, and au pair placements

SCOTLAND

Organisation Brackett Agency Ltd

Address 33B Heriot Row, Edinburgh EH3 6ES Tel 031-225 8768

Profile A commercial private organisation founded in 1966 to provide good family paying guest accommodation

Areas Edinburgh

Ages 17+, younger for accompanied children

Stay 1-4 weeks, all year

Language tuition Summer courses can be arranged for individuals

Activities Families often arrange outings; excursions arranged for groups

Accommodation Single/twin bedrooms in selected families. Each home is inspected to ensure accommodation is of a good standard.

Costs £56 bed and breakfast, £70 half board, per week

Escorted travel Can be arranged

Insurance Not provided

Other services Programmes for student groups

ENGLAND

Organisation The British Connection

Address 2 Lucas Close, Yateley, Camberley, Surrey GU17 7JD Tel Yateley 873705

Profile A commercial organisation founded in 1982 organising language courses and study programmes for multi-national groups, enabling young people from many different countries to meet and study together

Areas Berkshire, Hampshire and Surrey

Ages 12+

Stay Easter and summer, individuals; all year, groups.

Level of English required 2 years knowledge

Language tuition English courses arranged

Activities Family outings; courses include excursions, sports and social activities

Accommodation Great care is taken in visiting and selecting families. Single/twin bedrooms.

Costs £60 per week, full board

Escorted travel Special arrangements made for individuals, depending on age; couriers with coaches for groups from airports, stations or ports

Insurance Not provided

Other services Study programmes

H special arrangements made

ENGLAND & SCOTLAND

Organisation Castle Holiday Homes

Address 1 New Inn Lane, Guildford, Surrey GU4 7HN Tel Guildford 32345

Profile A private organisation founded in 1958 organising leisure and cultural activities

Areas Guildford, Woking, Bognor Regis, Southbourne, Chichester, Bournemouth, Christchurch, Havant, Petersfield, Oxford, Cambridge, Stirling, Perth and Dundee

Ages 10+

Stay 1+ weeks during holidays for individuals; 3+ days all year for groups

Level of English required Elementary

Language tuition English courses available at centres in Woking, Guildford, Southbourne and Chichester, July and August.

Activities Sports, excursions

Accommodation Single/twin/double bedrooms

Costs £75-£85 per week full board, individuals; £8 per day, short stay groups

Escorted travel Escort service provided from airport for under 18s. Coaches provided for group transfers if required.

Insurance Not provided

Other services Special activity courses for groups combining tennis, riding or watersports with English language lessons

Additional information Groups should apply at least 4 months in advance

H depending on host family

ENGLAND & SCOTLAND

Organisation Contacts In Britain

Address PO Box 10, Rye, East Sussex TN31 6BW Tel Rye 882444

Profile A commercial organisation founded in 1970 arranging linguistic and sightseeing stays in Europe. Offers a special service to overseas visitors wishing to learn English and acquaint themselves with the British way of life.

Areas London suburbs, Edinburgh, Shrewsbury, Kent, Sussex and other areas

Ages 10-60

Stay 1+ weeks, all year

Language tuition Can be arranged in certain locations at recommended English language schools. Private tuition also available.

Activities Excursions and sports tuition

Accommodation Families are carefully chosen for their suitability in receiving foreign visitors. Every effort is made to match visitors with families having similar interests and backgrounds.

Costs £60-£101 full board per week, depending on facilities. From £110, 10 days full board, groups. £2 surcharge per night for ages 21+. Registration fee £32.

Escorted travel Visitors are met by hosts at the nearest station. Escort from air/sea port can be arranged at extra cost.

Insurance Not provided

Other services Language courses, sports visits, specially prepared programmes for groups or individuals, linguistic and discovery homestay programmes for groups, and au pair placements

Additional information 24 hour telephone answering service to deal with any problems

H given sufficient notice

ENGLAND

Organisation Contactus

Address Elfin Lodge, Upper Hartfield, Sussex TN7 4AS Tel Hartfield 277418

Profile A private organisation founded in 1961 to promote friendship and a knowledge of life in England

Areas South east England

Ages 12+

Stay Weekly, all year

Level of English required Some knowledge helpful

Language tuition English courses and private lessons can be arranged

Accommodation Carefully selected families; each one is visited personally. Details of background and interests are matched between visitors and host families, and both receive full particulars before final arrangements are made.

Costs £75-£90 full board per week, depending on facilities offered. Registration fee £25.

Escorted travel Participants can be met at airport by host family on request

Insurance Not provided

ENGLAND & WALES

Organisation Country Cousins Ltd

Address Park School, Bicclescombe, Ilfracombe, Devon EX34 8JN Tel Ilfracombe 62834/63304

Profile A commercial organisation founded in 1956 arranging English language programmes and homestays in selected families

Areas Devon, Cornwall, Somerset, Herefordshire, Dorset, Wiltshire, Gloucestershire, Gwent and Powys

Ages All ages

Stay Usually 3 weeks, all year

Language tuition Available at language schools in Devon (for individuals) and in Devon and Somerset (groups), March-August

Activities Outings with the host family

Accommodation All families have teenage children, and have been visited and approved. The aim is to match age and interests of the guest with those of the family.

Costs £269 3 weeks full board

Escorted travel Escort service available from Heathrow, with escort coach service to the West Country

Insurance Not provided

Other services Language courses with excursions/activities, spring and summer

H

ENGLAND

Organisation Cultural Travel International Ltd

Address 13A Cranley Gardens, London SW7 3BB Tel 01-373 0791

Profile A commercial organisation founded in 1982, offering a student travel service

Areas Bournemouth, Canterbury, Harrogate, Tunbridge Wells, Worcester and London (Catford and Harrow)

Ages 12-23

Stay 2 days-4 weeks, all year

Language tuition None provided

Activities Outings may be arranged by the host family. Programmes arranged for groups.

Accommodation Families are carefully selected and have background and interests to fit in with those of the guests

Costs From £78-£98 per week, single room, full board, depending on location and facilities; half board also available. Special rates for groups.

Escorted travel Personal service by car from designated pick-up point can be arranged at extra cost. Coach transfer for groups.

Insurance Arranged on request

Other services Linguistic stays in summer and programmes of visits and excursions

BRITAIN

Organisation Dragons International

Address The Old Vicarage, South Newington, Banbury, Oxfordshire OX15 4JN Tel Banbury 721717

Profile A commercial organisation founded in 1975 enabling young people to spend 2/3 weeks living as a member of a family abroad on a homestay or exchange basis

Areas Throughout Britain

Ages 11-19

Stay 2/3 weeks, March-April, July-August

Level of English required Basic knowledge

Language tuition None provided

Activities Host family arranges outings

Accommodation Single or shared bedrooms in carefully selected families with young people of similar age or background

Costs £250 2 weeks

Escorted travel Escorted coach travel from a number of pick-up points in France, Germany and Spain provided

Insurance Provided

Other services Exchange visits

Overseas representation Dragons International, 4 rue de Port Marly, 78750 Mareil Marly, France Tel (3) 916 54 13

FIOCES

IRELAND & NORTHERN IRELAND

Organisation Dublin School of English

Address 10-12 Westmoreland Street, Dublin 2, Ireland Tel Dublin 773322

Profile A private school founded in 1968 promoting knowledge of other countries through fostering cultural stays on a homestay or au pair basis

Areas Throughout Ireland and Northern Ireland

Ages All ages

Stay 1+ weeks, all year

Language tuition Arranged on request

Activities Social, cultural and sporting events, excursions on vacation courses

Accommodation Carefully selected families, who are checked before students are allocated to them. Single/twin bedrooms.

Costs IR£95 Dublin area, IR£110 outside Dublin, UK£110 Northern Ireland, per week, half board

Escorted travel Students are collected from the airport and can be transferred to families or stations at extra cost

Insurance Not provided

Other services English language courses, general interest and sports holidays, group holiday language courses and au pair placements

IRELAND

Organisation Educational Facilities

Address 47 Castle Grove, Clontarf, Dublin 3, Ireland Tel Dublin 331005

Profile A private organisation founded in 1965 to teach English to foreign students and to give a knowledge and insight into Ireland and its people

Areas Dublin and Skerries, Co Dublin

Ages All ages

Stay As requested, all year

Language tuition Arrange English language programme inclusive of classes, cultural visits, excursions and family accommodation

Activities Visits to places of educational, artistic and cultural interest; optional sports programme

Accommodation Single bedrooms

Costs £60 per week half board, full board on request; administration fee £25

Escorted travel Students met at airport and introduced to families

Insurance Not provided

BRITAIN

Organisation Educational Travel Service

Address 82 Newlands Road, Norbury, London SW16 4SU Tel 01-679 8866

Profile A private organisation founded in 1968 arranging cultural, educational and holiday visits in the UK for groups, and accommodation in families for groups and individuals

Areas London, Canterbury, Eastbourne, Isle of Wight, Paignton, Cambridge, Edinburgh and the Lake District

Ages 14+

Stay 2+ nights, all year

Language tuition English courses can be arranged in London, Eastbourne and Paignton

Activities Excursions can be arranged for groups

Accommodation Host families are carefully selected. Single/twin bedrooms.

Costs From £53.55 bed and breakfast, £72.45 half board, £81.90 full board, per week

Escorted travel Detailed travel directions are given; escort can be arranged on request. Transport to families from local centres for groups.

Insurance Not provided

Other services Organise study tours for university/college groups on all subjects, inclusive of lectures and technical visits

Overseas representation Ball Tourist Services, Staufenstrasse 6, 4050 Moenchengladbach 1, Federal Republic of Germany Tel 34426

H London only

ENGLAND

Organisation Eduhols

Address PO Box 77, Sutton, Surrey Tel 01-642 5787

Profile A private organisation founded in 1958 to help overseas students to live as one of the family

Areas Bournemouth, Broadstone and Sutton

Ages 14+

Stay 2-4 weeks; all year

Language tuition English lessons can be arranged

Activities Families arrange outings

Accommodation Host families are carefully selected and visited regularly; descriptions of the family are sent to guests for approval. Single bedrooms.

Costs £133 full board, 2 weeks; £230 full board, 4 weeks

Escorted travel Not provided

Insurance Not provided

Other services Group holidays with English language lessons, leisure activities and excursions

ENGLAND

Organisation The Elizabeth Johnson Organisation

Address West House, 19/21 West Street, Haslemere, Surrey GU27 2AE
Tel Haslemere 52751

Profile A private organisation founded in 1957 to promote
communication and understanding between young people from all
walks of life both in Europe and worldwide

Areas Southern England, Heart of England and Cambridge

Ages 12+

Stay 1+ weeks, all year

Language tuition English courses arranged with family
accommodation, including social and excursion programme

Activities Excursions and activities can be arranged at extra cost

Accommodation Host families are chosen with great care and take a
genuine interest in guests, helping them to enjoy the English way of life.
Twin bedrooms; single room supplement.

Costs From £9.75 per day, full board; reductions for groups

Escorted travel Can arrange transfers from ports/airports

Insurance Can be arranged

Other services Language/special interest courses, adventure holiday
camps, sports and drama courses, band and choir tours and tailor-made
programmes

Additional information The local organiser keeps in close touch with
the families and students and is ready to assist should problems arise

H limited number

FIYTO

BRITAIN & IRELAND

Organisation Euro Academy Ltd

Address 77a George Street, Croydon, Surrey CR0 1LD Tel 01-681 2905

Profile A private organisation founded in 1971 to develop the relationships between young people throughout the world by bringing them together on both study and activity courses/visits

Areas Greater London, Canterbury, Oxford, Cambridge, Worthing, Bath, Exeter, Weston-super-Mare, York, Chester, Windsor, Guildford, Abergavenny, Edinburgh, Dublin and Cork

Ages 9-35

Stay Weekly, all year

Level of English required Knowledge of English not necessary but helps

Language tuition Arrange English language/activity courses

Activities Excursions and sports courses.

Accommodation Carefully selected families; single/twin bedrooms

Costs £72-£118 per week depending on location and facilities

Escorted travel Can be arranged

Insurance Not provided

Other services English language courses, sports courses and residential accommodation

FIYTO

BRITAIN

Organisation Eurolanguage Ltd

Address Greyhound House, 23/24 George Street, Richmond, Surrey TW9 1HY Tel 01-940 1087/948 5846

Profile A commercial organisation founded in 1972, concerned with the promotion of English life, culture and language

Areas All over Britain

Ages 8+

Stay 2+ weeks, all year

Language tuition Private tuition available; also option of attending family's local school

Activities Cultural and sports activities, excursions

Accommodation Host families are interviewed personally and are selected to match the needs, interests and background of each guest; close contact is maintained with them at all times. Single bedrooms.

Costs £220, 2 weeks full board

Escorted travel Escorts can be arranged from ports/airports to host families

Insurance Not provided

Other services English language courses, sports courses, childrens holidays, sightseeing visits, short study tours, tailor-made tours of Britain and academic year stays

H accepted

BRITAIN, IRELAND & CHANNEL ISLANDS

Organisation European Educational Opportunities Programme

Address 28 Canterbury Road, Lydden, Dover, Kent CT15 7ER Tel Dover 823631

Profile A non-profitmaking organisation founded in 1986 aiming to offer high-quality programmes through carefully selected homes, schools and allied agencies

Areas Throughout England, Wales, Ireland, and the Channel Islands (excluding June-September)

Ages Homestays 12+; term stays 16+

Stay Homestays 2+ weeks, all year; term stays spring, summer and winter terms

Level of English required Basic knowledge desirable

Language tuition English conversation available in most areas; homestays combined with formal tuition available in Kent and Sussex, Easter and summer

Activities Outings usually arranged by the families; homestays with organised excursions available for ages 15+

Accommodation Students are totally integrated into a family and in the case of term stays, attend a local school

Costs Homestays from £65 per week, full board; term stays £250 per month

Escorted travel Participants are met on arrival at Dover or Folkestone; escorted travel can be arranged from France or Germany

Insurance Not provided

Other services Term stays at independent boarding schools, class visits, city adventure and work experience programmes

Overseas representation France: ANEAS, 54 Grande Rue, 89113 Fleury la Vallee

Germany: Jeuneurope-Studienfahrten, Oststrasse 162, 4000 Dusseldorf 1

Additional information Students aged 12-18 are supervised by a member of staff; parents may telephone at any time to discuss problems or areas of concern

ENGLAND

Organisation Euroyouth Ltd

Address 301 Westborough Road, Westcliff-on-Sea, Essex SS0 9PT Tel 0702 341434

Profile A commercial organisation founded in 1961 with the aim of offering facilities for young people to practise the language which they are learning in a family setting and to experience the way of life of the country they are visiting

Areas Essex and London

Ages 14+

Stay Dates by arrangement

Level of English required Basic knowledge

Language tuition English language courses can be arranged; private tuition also available

Activities Family outings at extra cost. Sports courses in July and August; weekly day outings. Visits and programmes arranged for groups.

Accommodation Selected and inspected private homes; bed and breakfast, half or full board

Costs £50-£65 per week, depending on terms

Escorted travel Arranged on request at extra cost

Insurance Not provided; all guests must have personal liability insurance cover

Other services Tailor-made programmes for groups

Additional information Welfare service available; advice and assistance provided during stay for guests if required.

H limited opportunities

FIYTO FIOCES

BRITAIN & IRELAND

Organisation The Experiment in International Living

Address Otesaga, West Malvern Road, Upper Wyche, Malvern, Worcestershire WR14 4EN Tel Malvern 62577

Profile A non-profitmaking educational travel organisation founded in 1936 with the aim of promoting understanding, friendship and respect between people from different cultural backgrounds

Areas Throughout Britain and Ireland

Ages 16+

Stay 1-4 weeks, all year

Level of English required None necessary

Language tuition Courses can be arranged

Activities Families usually arrange outings. Activities and excursions included in group programmes. Professional courses arranged on request.

Accommodation Varies from single room to floor space, depending on family. Families are carefully selected with the understanding that the aim is to allow individuals to experience a different way of life; the circumstances and beliefs of the host family may therefore differ from those of the participants.

Costs £75 per week, full board; travel extra. Occasional grant aid available on some programmes.

Escorted travel Group travel arrangements made; arrangements for individuals on request. Host families will meet participants at airport/station if requested.

Insurance Provided

Other services Special interest and UK/US high school programmes

Overseas representation Over 45 offices worldwide: details from UK office

Additional information Apply 8-10 weeks in advance

H with advance notification

BRITAIN

Organisation Families in Britain

Address Martins Cottage, Martins Lane, Birdham, Chichester, Sussex PO20 7AU Tel Chichester 512222

Profile A commercial company founded in 1960 specialising in introducing overseas visitors to private families

Areas Throughout Britain

Ages All ages

Stay Weekly, all year

Level of English required Basic knowledge an advantage

Language tuition English lessons on a private basis or at a language school can be arranged

Activities Host families organise visits to London and local places of interest

Accommodation Families are carefully selected by matching ages, interests, hobbies and background

Costs £70-£100 half board, £90-£120 full board, per week. Registration fee £10.

Escorted travel Visitors can be met at air/sea ports at extra cost

Insurance Not included

Other services Sports and special interest courses

Overseas representation Federal Republic of Germany: S&H Deyerlei, Eichhornchenweg 3, 2080 Pinneberg Tel 04101/61744 (10.00-20.00 hours)

Spain: Petrina Murray, Residencial Horizonte No 30 (3o, 1o), Majadahonda, Madrid Tel 91-638-7334

Additional information Maximum size of groups: 8 persons

H depending on disability

BRITAIN

Organisation Family Holidays

Address 42 Walton Road, Sidcup, Kent DA14 4LN Tel 01-300 5444

Profile A commercial organisation founded in 1968 providing an opportunity for overseas visitors to experience lifewith a British family

Areas Throughout Britain

Ages All ages

Stay 1+ weeks, individuals; 2+ days, groups; all year.

Accommodation A list of 250 British families is sent on request to applicants who select family and location. Single/twin/family bedrooms.

Costs £70 half board, £82.35 full board, per week. Half price for children under 10; group rates on request. Booking fee £10.

Escorted travel Escorts can be arranged; groups are met at airports or pick-up points

Insurance Not provided

H Handicapped families are included on host family list, and are equipped to deal with handicapped guests

ENGLAND & CHANNEL ISLANDS

Organisation FERN

Address 105 Gordon Road, Camberley, Surrey GU15 2JQ Tel
Camberley 27033

Profile A private, commercial organisation founded in 1961 with the
aim of introducing young students of all nations, creeds and colours to
England and the English people

Areas Camberley, Chichester, St Albans and St Helier (Jersey)

Ages 11+

Stay 2+ weeks, all year

Language tuition Individual courses for students available, Easter and
May-October

Activities Sports, cultural visits and excursions

Accommodation All students stay with carefully selected and visited
host families

Costs £125 per week full board, fully inclusive

Escorted travel Students are met at main London airports or rail
stations

Insurance Arranged on request

Other services Business English courses and specialist tours for
choirs/school bands

Additional information Office open 24 hours to deal with any
problems which may arise; a liaison officer is present at each centre to
assist in cases of difficulty between students and host families

H accepted

ENGLAND

Organisation German Student Holidays/West Country Student Holidays

Address Little Bias, Croyde, Braunton, Devon EX33 1QE Tel Croyde 890352

Profile A commercial organisation founded in 1978, organising educational holidays in England for German and Italian students

Areas North and south Devon, Cotswolds, Worcester, Vale of Evesham

Ages 10-30+

Stay 2-8 weeks

Level of English required Basic knowledge

Language tuition English tuition individually or in small groups on request

Activities Group excursions; families are expected to organise weekend excursions

Accommodation Families are personal friends or listed through personal recommendation, and are mostly professional or farming families; considerable trouble is taken to match students. Single bedrooms.

Costs Approx £100 per week full board, including weekend excursions

Escorted travel Students collected from airport with personal escort service to families

Insurance provided on request

Overseas representation Federal Republic of Germany: Beissner Touristik International, Brabeckstrasse 15A, 3000 Hannover; Frau Anna von Gleichen, Goethestrasse 23, bei Allzeit, 6000 Frankfurt/Main; Frau Christa Michaelis, Hampsteadstrasse 23A, 1000 Berlin 37; Frau Anna-Maria van Lossow, Klosterrather Weg 10, 5303 Bornheim-Hersel

Italy: Signora Valeria Carati, via Gualandi 13, Bologna 40137

Additional information 24 hour, 7 day emergency and enquiry service. Limited accommodation for parents accompanying their children.

ENGLAND

Organisation Gesellschaft fur Internationale Jugendkontakte eV

Address Am Helpert 32-34, Postfach 200 562, 5300 Bonn 2, Federal Republic of Germany Tel 32 26 49

Profile A non-profitmaking organisation founded in 1983, arranging homestays and exchanges

Areas London and Norwich

Ages 13+

Stay 1-4 weeks, Easter and summer

Level of English required Fair knowledge preferable but not essential

Language tuition Optional English courses can be arranged

Activities Excursions arranged with English courses

Accommodation All families are visited and carefully selected, and are matched with guests according to background, hobbies, interests and location

Costs From DM465 1 week, DM845 2 weeks, DM1385 4 weeks, full board; half board also available in London

Escorted travel Can be arranged

Insurance Can be arranged

Other services Exchanges, summer schools and courses, au pair placements and guides on work and study opportunities for young people

SCOTLAND

Organisation Hobby Holidays

Address Glencommon, Inchmarlo, Banchory, Kincardineshire Tel Banchory 2628

Profile A commercial organisation founded in 1975 to promote individually planned activity or language/culture holidays for independent visitors

Areas Deeside

Ages 8-18

Stay 1+ weeks, all year; school groups in May/June and September/October

Level of English required A little knowledge necessary

Language tuition English lessons available

Activities Sports, excursions and activities

Accommodation Single/twin bedrooms

Costs From £75 per week full board

Escorted travel Transfers to and from airport

Insurance Not provided

Other services Farmstays, multi-activity and pony camp weeks

H but site prevents wheelchair access

ENGLAND

Organisation Host & Guest Service

Address 592A King's Road, London SW6 2DX Tel 01-731 5340

Profile A private organisation founded in 1956, providing a wide variety of reliable accommodation with families according to individual needs

Areas London and suburbs, Brighton, Canterbury, York and Manchester

Ages All ages; young children will need to be accompanied by an adult

Stay To suit individual requirements

Language tuition Details of local language school provided on request

Activities Families may arrange outings on request

Accommodation Offer an individual service ensuring compatibility of host and guest; young people are placed in homes with young people of similar interests.

Costs £40-£80 bed & breakfast, £60-£90 half board, £70-£120 full board, per week. Service charge £30; £10 for stays of less than 10 days.

Escorted travel Adults are met at local stations; young people can be met at airport/station at extra cost

Insurance Arranged on request

Other services Au pair placements

H placed where possible

ENGLAND & IRELAND

Organisation Inter Sejours

Address 4 rue de Parme, 75009 Paris, France Tel 42 80 09 38 and 179 rue de Courcelles, 75017 Paris, France Tel 47 63 06 81

Profile A non-profitmaking organisation founded in 1968, arranging homestays, linguistic stays and au pair placements

Areas London, Cornwall and Cork, and on farms throughout England

Ages 14+

Stay 2+ weeks, all year

Language tuition Combined homestay/language course available

Activities Outings arranged by families

Accommodation Information about the host family is sent to the participant, so that correspondence can take place beforehand if desired. Single or shared bedrooms.

Costs From FF2200 (London, 2 weeks) to FF3000 (Cork, 3 weeks), full board

Escorted travel Transfers by arrangement

Insurance Provided

Other services Combined homestay/language/activity holidays and au pair placements

BRITAIN

Organisation International Catholic Service for Homestays & Penfriends

Address Veilchenweg 2, 6634 Wallerfangen, Federal Republic of Germany Tel 60638

Profile A voluntary non-profitmaking organisation founded in 1950, offering a paying guest service .

Areas Towns and villages throughout Britain

Ages 12-25

Stay 2-4 weeks Christmas/Easter, and 15 June-30 September

Level of English required Minimum 2 years study

Accommodation In selected friendly, hospitable and Christian families

Costs DM300-DM1070 full board, depending on family and length of stay. Registration fee DM70.

Escorted travel Not provided

Insurance Included

Other services Penfriend service

Additional information Character references required; applicants must be students or undertaking vocational training. Apply at least 4 weeks in advance.

ENGLAND

Organisation Interspeak Ltd

Address 14 Robin Hill Drive, Standish, near Wigan, Greater Manchester WN6 0QW Tel Standish 421960

Profile A commercial organisation founded in 1981 to provide good family accommodation for foreign students and to improve international relations among young people

Areas Blackpool, Southport, Manchester, York and London

Ages 12+

Stay April-October, individuals; April-August, groups

Level of English required Basic knowledge helpful

Language tuition Combined homestay/language courses available

Activities Family outings; organised activities available as part of the language course

Accommodation Single bedroom in family with teenage children where possible

Costs £85 per week full board

Escorted travel Travel in groups from south west France via Paris to north west England possible, April-August. Participants can be met at Manchester airport at extra cost.

Insurance Not provided

Other services Exchange visits, language holidays and French cookery courses

Overseas representation VECSI, 10 rue Ludovic Trarieux, 16007 Angouleme, France Tel 95 73 57

H accepted

ENGLAND

Organisation Island Welcome

Address 2 Castle Road, Wroxall, Isle of Wight PO38 3DU Tel Ventnor 853403

Profile A commercial organisation founded in 1979 providing a personalised homestay service

Areas Isle of Wight

Ages 13-70, younger if accompanied

Stay Individuals all year except July; groups all year

Level of English required Basic English necessary for individuals

Language tuition English language classes for groups on request

Activities Excursions and social activities; sports and activities on request

Accommodation Families are carefully selected, and homes regularly inspected. Single/twin bedrooms.

Costs £42 bed and breakfast, £56 half board, £63 full board, per week. Reductions for groups.

Escorted travel Available for groups at extra cost

Insurance Not provided

ENGLAND & WALES

Organisation Language & Leisure Services

Address 228A High Street, Bromley, Kent BR1 1PQ Tel 01-460 4861

Aims A private organisation founded in 1959 to enable and encourage young people from overseas to come to England at realistic cost and to learn about England, its way of life, language and culture

Areas London suburbs, Kent, Surrey, Sussex, Essex, Hampshire, Dorset, Devon, Cornwall and Wales

Ages 13+

Stay 2+ weeks, all year

Level of English required Elementary knowledge and upwards

Language tuition English classes can be arranged

Activities Participants share in family activities

Accommodation The emphasis is on a genuine welcome and interest on the part of the host family

Costs From £67.50 per week, half board; full board available

Escorted travel Can be arranged

Insurance Not provided

Other services English language summer courses, study tours of London and boarding and day school scheme

ENGLAND

Organisation Linden Bureau

Address 68 Deanecroft Road, Eastcote, Pinner, Middlesex HA5 1SP Tel 01-866 5435

Aims A private organisation founded in 1966, placing overseas visitors in families with an emphasis on personal attention

Areas London (Pinner, Harrow, Ealing and Acton) and Eastbourne area

Ages 15/16+

Stay 1+ weeks, all year

Level of English required Knowledge of English preferred

Language tuition Can provide advice on courses

Activities Excursions sometimes arranged by the host family

Accommodation Single/shared bedrooms

Costs £65 bed and breakfast, £70 half board, £75 full board, per week

Escorted travel Not provided

Insurance Not provided

Overseas representation France: ICO, 55 rue de Rivoli, 75001 Paris

Italy: ARCE, via Garibaldi 20 (primo piano), 16124 Genova

Spain: Associacion Internacional Cultural Au-Pair, Paseo de Gracia, 86, 6o 7a, 08008 Barcelona

Portugal: Mrs M Noemia Carvalho, Rua Antonio Jose da Costa 47, 4100 Porto

Switzerland: Mrs Ingrid Wilson, rue de la Promenade, 2105 Travers (Neuchatel)

ENGLAND

Organisation Mauder Associates

Address PO Box 11, Halstead, Essex CO9 1TT Tel Halstead 472957

Profile A commercial organisation founded in 1971 with the aim of helping foreign guests to learn English in the environment of an English family

Areas Mainly Essex, Suffolk and Kent

Ages 13-68

Stay Any length, all year

Level of English required General knowledge necessary

Language tuition Not provided

Activities Families arrange outings

Accommodation Details of suitable families are sent to guests for selection. Single bedrooms.

Costs £50 bed and breakfast, £60 half board, £70-£110 full board, per week. Agency fee £30-£50 depending on length of stay.

Escorted travel Some families collect from ports, rail stations and airports at extra charge. Also across-London escort, escorting guests from arrival to departure stations, then informing host family which train to meet.

Insurance Not provided

IRELAND

Organisation Morrissey Linguistic Centre Ltd

Address Valhall, Killinure, Athlone, Co Westmeath, Ireland Tel Athlone 85160

Profile A commercial organisation founded in 1969 organising language courses, homestays, farmstays and riding programmes

Areas Athlone, Longford, Roscommon, Birr, Moate

Ages 9-18

Stay Homestays 3/4 weeks; farmstays 3/4/6 weeks

Level of English required None necessary

Language tuition Courses available on request

Activities Weekly coach excursions; full sports facilities and programmes

Accommodation Family accommodation in private homes and farms

Costs £80 per week, full board

Escorted travel Escort to and from airport and central meeting point arranged

Insurance Provided

Other services English courses and riding programmes

Additional information A limited number of places are available for foreign students wishing to attend primary or secondary school for a term or year

BRITAIN

Organisation Naturfreundejugend Deutschlands

Address Intercultur, Rosenstrasse 1, 4806 Werther, Federal Republic of Germany Tel (0) 5203-5109/5204-5711

Profile A voluntary non-profitmaking organisation founded in 1895 to offer cultural experience and political education to working people. It provides a service in particular for the less well-off and the socially disadvantaged.

Areas Throughout Britain

Ages No limits

Stay 1-3 weeks, all year

Level of English required None necessary

Language tuition None provided

Activities Host families are not obliged to arrange anything but careful matching ensures that host and guest share similar interests

Accommodation Varies from single room to floor space for sleeping bag, depending on family. Hosts and guests are matched carefully with particular attention given to knowledge of languages; the emphasis is on guests being treated as visitors and not paying guests. Meals provided by mutual arrangement.

Costs Hosts and guests arrange contribution to household expenses, approx DM70 per week. Agency fee DM100.

Escorted travel Not provided

Insurance Not provided

UK representation Mrs S Kortlandt, Intercultur, 91 Marlborough Gardens, Upminster, Essex RM14 1SQ Tel Upminster 25617

H

ENGLAND

Organisation Osterreichische Vereinigung fur Austausch und Studienreisen (OVAST)

Address Dr Gschmeidlerstrasse 10/4, 3500 Krems, PO Box 148, Austria Tel 02732 5743

Profile A non-profitmaking organisation founded in 1964 arranging homestays and exchanges

Areas London and Brighton

Ages Mainly 10-20

Stay 18/25 days, June-August

Language tuition Optional English classes available as part of the programme

Activities Outings and social activities arranged

Accommodation In selected families

Costs AS10118 18 days, AS11445 25 days, full board plus AS550 enrolment fee

Escorted travel By train provided; extra for escorted air travel

Insurance Provided

Other services Class visits for Austrian schools (ages 14-17) on homestay or exchange basis with children attending school, home-to-home exchanges, summer schools and language courses

FIYTO FIOCES

BRITAIN

Organisation Project Tours International/Student Accommodation Services

Address 67 Wigmore Street, London W1H 9LG Tel 01-935 9979

Profile A commercial organisation founded in 1969, aiming to provide economical accommodation in private homes, hostels and hotels, for students and visitors

Areas Mainly London, but also in Bath, Cambridge, Inverness, Oxford, Southport and York

Ages 16+

Stay 1+ weeks, all year; shorter stays possible in London

Language tuition English courses available in London

Activities None arranged for individuals

Accommodation Care is taken to match host and guest, and homes are carefully inspected; single/shared bedrooms

Costs From £44-£63 bed & breakfast, from £58-£88 half board

Escorted travel Not provided

Insurance Not provided

Other services Also arrange hostel and hotel accommodation, and special interest stays, for groups

ENGLAND

Organisation The Robertson Organisation

Address 44 Willoughby Road, London NW3 1RU Tel 01-435 4907

Profile A private organisation founded in 1948 to promote language learning and understanding among young people of Europe

Areas North and north west London

Ages 11-21

Stay 2-3 weeks Easter and July/August

Level of English required 1 years study

Language tuition Not provided

Activities Programme of visits, outings and sports

Accommodation Single/twin bedrooms in carefully selected families, usually with children of the same age/sex

Costs From £275 2 weeks, from £365 3 weeks, full board

Escorted travel Provided for groups; individuals can link up with a group in Paris at extra cost, or be met at airport

Insurance Can be arranged

Other services Arrange exchange visits

Overseas representation L'Organisation Robertson, 51 rue de la Harpe, 75005 Paris, France Tel 46 33 12 89

Additional information Prefer to meet applicants and parents; appointments can be booked

H depending on nature of handicap

FIOCES

BRITAIN

Organisation Studentours

Address 3 Harcourt Street, London W1H 1DS Tel 01-402 5131/2/3

Profile A commercial organisation founded in 1965, providing reasonably priced accommodation in families, residential centres and student hotels, which can be combined with language tuition, sports and special activities

Areas London and throughout Britain

Ages 7+

Stay Any length, all year

Language tuition English courses available

Activities Outings arranged by host family. Educational journeys, field studies, music and sports, depending on programme.

Accommodation Twin bedrooms

Costs £7 per night bed & breakfast, £9 per night half board, £10 per night full board. Weekly reductions for groups.

Escorted travel Not provided

Insurance Provided on request

Other services Special interest tours and educational journeys, field studies, band/choir visits and special courses for school groups

H at student centres in Sussex and Kent

FIYTO FIOCES

BRITAIN

Organisation The Travel-at-Home Family Bureau

Address Craighall, Huntly, Aberdeenshire AB5 4QN Tel Kennethmont 215

Profile A private business founded in 1975 which finds carefully selected host families for those coming to Britain to improve their knowledge of English and have a good holiday

Areas Mainly country households in England, Scotland and Wales

Ages 8+

Stay 2/3+ weeks, all year

Language tuition English lessons can be arranged

Activities Cultural and sports activities as part of the programme

Accommodation Families are chosen to match the guests, with regard to background, interests, hobbies and personality, as far as possible. Guests can share room with same-age child of family, if wished. The accent is on making the visit useful and instructive, with complete immersion in family life.

Costs £120-£140 per week full board, including excursions and entrance tickets; half board also available. £25 introduction fee.

Escorted travel Hosts meet guests at airport or suitable point

Insurance Not provided

H possible

SCOTLAND

Organisation UK Scottish Connection

Address 1 Durham Terrace, Edinburgh EH15 1QJ Tel 031-669 3115

Profile A private organisation founded in 1971 providing young visitors with comfortable accommodation in selected families, where help and encouragement is given to guests to speak English

Areas Edinburgh, St Andrews, Inverness

Ages 14+

Stay Weekly, all year

Level of English required Some knowledge an advantage

Language tuition Can arrange English courses

Activities Excursions for groups; cultural activities includes Festival programme in August

Accommodation All families are personally visited and selected, chosen for comfort, friendliness and hospitality

Costs From £70 per week full board, groups; costs for individuals on request

Escorted travel Guests can be met at Edinburgh arrival point

Insurance Not provided

H in limited homes

BRITAIN & IRELAND

Organisation Visit Britain

Address Studio 23, Udimore Road, Rye, East Sussex TN31 7DS Tel Rye 224871

Profile A commercial organisation founded in 1984 offering holidays, homestays, farmstays and courses

Areas England, Scotland, Wales and Ireland; mainly south east England for young visitors

Ages 7/8-80

Stay Any length, all year

Level of English required A little English helpful

Language tuition Individual tuition available in some areas

Activities Local outings and sports can often be arranged. Some hosts can provide transport and a guide service to places of interest.

Accommodation Carefully selected families, usually with teenage children. Each homestay is made on a personal basis, matching the requirements of visitors with the host families.

Costs From £65 half board, £110 full board, per week, depending on type of accommodation and facilities. Registration fee £25.

Escorted travel Visitors can be met at ports/airports, with car/rail escort to family

Insurance Not provided

Other services Language courses and individually planned itineraries

H where hosts' homes are suitable

BRITAIN & IRELAND

Organisation Youth Foreign Holiday Service

Address 96 St Blaize Road, Romsey, Hampshire SO51 7LW Tel Romsey 517626

Profile A non-profitmaking organisation founded in 1960, providing accommodation with friendly English families whose aim is to help overseas students improve their spoken English

Areas SE/SW London, Margate, Ramsgate, Brighton, Bournemouth, Weymouth, Torbay area, Penzance, Minehead area, Edinburgh and Dublin

Ages 15+

Stay Any length, all year

Level of English required Reasonable knowledge of English preferred

Activities Outings usually arranged by host family; excursions and activities can be arranged for small groups

Accommodation All homes are visited to ensure their suitability. Single/twin bedrooms.

Costs From £50 per week, half board, shared room; full board also available

Escorted travel Most families meet their guests at the local station

Insurance Not provided

FIYTO

HOMESTAYS
WORLDWIDE

UNITED STATES

Organisation American Institute for Foreign Study Scholarship Foundation

Address 37 Queen's Gate, London SW7 5HR Tel 01-581 2733

Profile The American Institute for Foreign Study (AIFS) was founded in 1964 to provide study and travel programmes for teachers and students interested in learning about other cultures. The AIFS Scholarship Foundation is a non-profitmaking organisation established in 1968 to promote international understanding through cross-cultural exchange. The Homestay in America programme enables students from overseas to live with an American family and to learn first-hand about life in the US.

Areas Boston, Chicago, Los Angeles, Miami, New York, Philadelphia, Portland, Providence, San Diego, San Francisco, Seattle, Washington DC

Ages 13-21

Stay 1-4 weeks, all year

Level of English required No specific level

Language tuition Various language/culture courses and intensive English courses available

Activities Family outings and planned activities three times a week, plus optional activities

Accommodation In carefully selected host families living within a 100 mile radius of a major city; possible to stay in 1 rural and 1 urban area for ages 17-21 on 3/4 week programmes. Single/shared bedrooms.

Costs From $310-$560, 1-4 weeks full board, plus travel costs

Escorted travel Transfer to/from airport

Insurance Health and accident insurance provided

Other services Au pair programme

US representation AIFS Scholarship Foundation, 100 Greenwich Avenue, Greenwich, Connecticut 06830

Additional information Individual applications accepted but the programme caters predominantly for groups

H cases considered individually

CANADA & UNITED STATES

Organisation Anglia International En Famille Homestay Agency

Address 154 Fronks Road, Dovercourt, Harwich, Essex CO12 4EF Tel Harwich 503717

Profile A private commercial organisation founded in 1983, arranging homestays for young people and adults

Areas Throughout Canada and the US

Ages 10+

Stay Weekly, all year

Accommodation Host families provide personal references which are taken up, and great importance is placed on these. Families and guests are matched according to interests and hobbies.

Costs £25-£30 per day, bed and breakfast, shared room; agency fee £19

Escorted travel Can be provided

Insurance Arranged on request

UNITED STATES

Organisation British American Schools Exchange Club (BASEC)

Address Kevin Shannon Travel Ltd, 38 Shepherds Bush Road, London W6 7PJ Tel 01-602 1390

Profile A commercial organisation founded in 1974 to promote cultural visits and exchanges for the benefit of young people, giving them the opportunity to experience family life in a foreign country. America at Home holidays offer opportunities to live with American families, taking a look at the social, economic and political influences in the US, and to enjoy everyday American life.

Areas East Coast, Florida and California

Ages 13-17

Stay 2/3 weeks, Easter and summer

Activities Cultural programme during the week with sightseeing and visits to schools; weekends spent with host family

Accommodation Full board with volunteer host families

Costs £500-£750 per person inclusive of travel, insurance and cultural programme

Escorted travel All travel arrangements made

Insurance Can be arranged

Other services Educational programmes with homestay visits for teachers to the US, Far East and Egypt on a rota basis every 2/3 years

WORLDWIDE

Organisation The Experiment in International Living

Address Otesaga, West Malvern Road, Upper Wyche, Malvern, Worcestershire WR14 4EN Tel Malvern 62577

Profile A non-profitmaking educational travel organisation founded in 1936 with the aim of promoting understanding, friendship and respect between people from different cultural backgrounds

Areas Africa: Kenya   Asia: Hong Kong, India, Japan, Korea, Malaysia, Nepal, Philippines, Singapore, Thailand
Australasia: Australia, New Zealand   Middle East: Israel, Turkey
North America: Canada, Hawaii, Martinique, Mexico, United States
South America: Argentina, Brazil, Chile, Ecuador, Uruguay

Ages 16+

Stay 1-4 weeks, all year

Level of language required None necessary

Language tuition Courses can be arranged

Activities Families usually arrange outings. Activities and excursions included in group programmes. Professional courses on request.

Accommodation Varies from single room to floor space, depending on country and family. Families are carefully selected with the understanding that the aim is to allow individuals to experience a different way of life; the circumstances and beliefs of the host family may therefore differ from those of the participants.

Costs From £82-£168 per week, depending on country; travel extra. Occasional grant aid available on some programmes.

Escorted travel Group travel arrangements made; arrangements for individuals on request. Host families will meet participants if requested.

Insurance Provided

Other services Special interest, UK/US high school and US au pair programmes

Overseas representation Over 45 offices worldwide

Additional information Apply 8-10 weeks in advance

H with advance notification

KOREA

Organisation KIYSES (Korea International Youth & Student Exchange Society)

Address Room 505, YMCA Building, Chongro 2 ka, Chongro-ku, Seoul, Korea Tel 732-6646/7

Profile A non-profitmaking organisation founded in 1974 to give youth and students valuable experience and knowledge within the international community

Areas Korea

Ages 18-40

Stay 2/3/7 days

Level of language required Some knowledge useful

Language tuition Courses arranged at extra cost

Activities Sightseeing and educational tours

Accommodation Korean-style meals and accommodation (mattress and blanket)

Costs US$30 per night, US$150 per week, bed and breakfast; half board available

Escorted travel Special arrangements on request

Insurance Not provided

Other services Provide complete educational travel services for local and foreign students/youth and, a counselling department for information on academic and language studies

BRAZIL

Organisation ML Turismo

Address Rua Gomes Carneiro 134, Casa 3, 22071 Ipanema, Rio de Janeiro, Brazil Tel 267 4688

Profile A commercial organisation founded in 1977, specialising in student and youth travel

Areas All major cities of Brazil including Sao Paulo, Rio de Janeiro, Brasilia, Porto Alegre, Recife, Manaus, Forta Leza, Salvador and Curitiba

Ages 15-36

Stay 1-28 days

Level of language required None necessary

Language tuition Portuguese courses can be arranged

Activities Outings arranged by host families. 10% discount on tours within Brazil to ISTC/FIYTO card holders.

Accommodation Bed and breakfast accommodation with a host family; single/shared bedrooms

Costs Approx US$10 per day

Escorted travel Participants can be met at the airport; escorts available for groups

Insurance Provided

Other services Exchanges, language courses, Amazon ecological tours

H special arrangements

FIYTO

UNITED STATES, JAPAN

Organisation World Exchange

Address World Exchange, White Birch Road, Box 377, Putnam Valley, NY 10579, US Tel (914) 526 2505/528 1981

Profile A non-profitmaking organisation founded in 1985 arranging homestays and exchanges with the aim of improving cross-cultural understanding between people of all ages and all nations

Areas United States: Putnam Valley, New York, East Coast, West Coast and Florida

Japan: Hitachi, Yokohama, Kamakura

Ages 13-21

Stay 1 month, July/August

Level of language/English required Minimum 2 years' study of English; no knowledge of Japanese required, but applicants are expected to learn about and have an interest in Japanese culture
Language tuition Can be arranged for groups

Activities One full-day, one half-day trip/event, plus farewell party arranged for groups of 20 or more. In the US activities are arranged by individual host families; in Japan lectures and demonstrations of traditional arts are organised.

Accommodation Full board; single/twin bedrooms in family home

Costs US: $360 per month, plus travel

Japan: $1,975 inclusive of travel, ex US

Escorted travel Students met at airport, taken to their area by bus and met by families

Insurance Not provided

Representation World Exchange, 2-24-20, Higashi Kanesawa Cho, Hitachi-Shi, Ibaraki-ken, Japan Tel (294) 32 2424

Additional information Host families are carefully selected and interviewed to ensure suitability

H accepted on US programme in association with PHAB

JAPAN

Organisation Young Abroad Club

Address Kowa Building 4th floor 2-3-12, Shinjuku, Shinjuku-Ku Tokyo 160, Japan Tel 03-341-8989

Profile A non-profitmaking organisation founded in 1971 to cultivate international understanding among young people. The Home Life in Japan programme is intended to provide young people from overseas with an experience of Japanese home life, while providing the Japanese hosts with the opportunity of speaking a foreign language.

Areas Japan

Ages 18-30

Stay 1 or 2 months possibly longer, all year

Level of language required None necessary

Accommodation Visitors are welcomed and integrated as a member of the Japanese family

Costs Board and lodging free in return for 15 hours English or other language tuition per week

Escorted travel Not provided

Insurance Not provided

Other services Arrange exchange visits

Additional information Applicants are introduced through the Club Bulletin and receive invitation letters from families interested in welcoming them; it is then up to the individual to make further arrangements. Applicants able to offer reciprocal hospitality for 1+ weeks will be more likely to find a suitable host.

EXCHANGES

BRITAIN/IRELAND: FRANCE

Organisation Amitie Internationale des Jeunes

Address Beaver House, 10a Woodborough Road, London SW15 6QA
Tel 01-788 6857

Profile A private commercial organisation founded in 1947 aiming to promote friendship between young people and their families and the improvement of language skills

Areas Throughout Britain, Ireland and France

Matching Applications are dealt with individually, and applicants with similar ages, interests and background are carefully matched

Ages 10-18/19

Stay 2-3 weeks, Christmas, Easter and summer

Level of language required One year's knowledge

Activities Families outline activities envisaged on the application form

Accommodation Full board; single/shared bedrooms .

Costs £94.20-£121.50 covers insurance, agency fees, and return travel London/Paris. Under reciprocal arrangements families may be requested to cover the child's travel London/Paris to the host family.

Travel By boat/train and coach; escorted Paris/London, where participants are met by the host families

Insurance Medical and personal liability insurance provided

Representation Amitie Internationale des Jeunes, 33 avenue d'Eylau, 75116 Paris, France Tel 47 27 75 64

Additional information Summer exchanges are the most popular with French families. Each child receives/visits during a holiday period, and visits/receives during the following vacation; during the summer the visits are immediately consecutive. The holiday may not always be spent in the French family's permanent town of residence. School reference and medical certificate required.

BRITAIN: AUSTRIA

Organisation Anglo-Austrian Society

Address 46 Queen Anne's Gate, London SW1H 9AU Tel 01-222 0366

Profile A non-protfitmaking charity founded in 1944 to promote educational and cultural exchange between Britain and Austria

Areas Throughout Britain and Austria

Matching Applicants are carefully selected and matched according to age, hobbies, interests and schooling. References are taken up and first consideration is given in choosing the right partner.

Ages 12-18

Stay 2/3/4 weeks, Easter and summer

Level of language required Some knowledge helpful, but not essential

Activities Visitors are included in all family outings and activities

Costs £154 inclusive; some £75 travel bursaries available

Travel Escorted parties from all parts of Britain to all parts of Austria; participants are then personally introduced to the respective families

Insurance Provided

Representation Anglo-Austrian Society, Stubenring 24, 1010 Vienna, Austria Tel 512 98 03/4

Other services Language courses and special interest holidays

Additional information Exchanges can be arranged over 2 years, but usually only for younger applicants

BRITAIN: FRANCE

Organisation Aquitaine Service Linguistique

Address 15 Allee des Genets, Domaine de Terre-Rouge, 33127 Martignas, France Tel 56 21 40 96

Profile A non-profitmaking organisation founded in 1978 arranging homestays, exchange visits and language courses

Areas Britain: Leicester area

France: all areas

Matching Applicants are carefully selected to match interests and background

Ages 16-18

Stay 2/3 weeks, July and August

Level of language required All levels accepted

Activities Cultural/sports facilities available in most areas

Accommodation Full board; single/shared bedrooms

Costs FF820 plus FF180 membership fee

Travel Help given with travel arrangements; participants are usually met by the host family

Insurance Provided for stays in Britain, but not in France

Other services Language courses and au pair placements; exchanges between France/US

UK representation Baxter's Agency & School of English, PO Box 12, Peterborough, Cambridgeshire PE3 6JN Tel Peterborough 62744/53463

Additional information The exchange can sometimes be completed at Easter of the following year

BRITAIN: SWEDEN

Organisation ASSET - Anglo Swedish State Educational Travel

Address 6 Harcourt Street, London W1H 2BD Tel 01-724 0280

Profile A non-profitmaking organisation established in 1938 by the Swedish government, promoting educational travel and international contacts and understanding between young people

Areas Throughout Britain and Sweden

Matching Applicants are carefully matched according to interests and hobbies

Ages 12-18

Stay 3 weeks July, Britain; 2/3 weeks July/August, Sweden

Level of language required None necessary

Activities Families are encouraged to arrange outings at weekends

Accommodation Full board; single/shared bedrooms

Costs £79 inclusive of travel and health insurance

Travel Escorted return travel from many pickup points by coach and boat, returning by air

Insurance Health insurance provided

Representation ASSE, Box 2017, Stockholm, Sweden

Other services Arrange a year in an American high school

Additional information Group leaders are on call throughout the stay. Exchanges are immediately consecutive, the British host returning to Sweden with the Swedish partner. Matchings are made in the spring. Approval will be sought from schools to allow the Swedish partner to attend school while in Britain. Early application advised.

H every effort made to accommodate

BRITAIN: FRANCE

Organisation Association pour les Voyages Educatifs (AVE)/ Maison de Cambridge

Address 1 rue General Riu, 34000 Montpellier, France Tel 67 64 07 86

Profile A non-profitmaking voluntary organisation arranging homestays, schooling abroad and exchanges. AVE is an educational visit/exchange organisation founded in 1984; Maison de Cambridge, founded in 1978 as the Centre Britannique, is a British cultural centre set up in 1985 by members of the local education authorities in Montpellier and Cambridge as part of Community Link.

Areas France: Montpellier, Nimes, Beziers, Sete, Aix-en-Provence

Britain: Cambridge, Peterborough and Northern Ireland

Matching Partners are matched on the basis of age, sex, hobbies, interests and social background

Ages 13-18

Stay 2 weeks, Easter; 3 weeks, summer

Level of language required Elementary

Activities Individual families may organise some activities

Accommodation Full board in single bedrooms

Costs £6 annual subscription fee; £150-£300 for travel, depending on point of departure, plus insurance and overheads

Travel Groups of children travel together by air, rail or coach, escorted by 1 participating teacher

Insurance Holiday risk/cancellation insurance provided

Representation Community Education Department, Shire Hall, Cambridge/Montpellier Exchange Register, Rainey Endowed School, Magherafelt, Northern Ireland

Other services Homestays and schooling abroad, au pair placements and working holidays

Additional information To ensure that visiting children do not speak too much of their own language no courses, activities or excursions are arranged after the initial group travel

BRITAIN: ITALY

Organisation Associazione Palermo Ospita

Address c/o Agata Greco, via Trentacoste 50, 90143 Palermo, Italy Tel 306927

Profile A voluntary non-profitmaking organisation founded in 1979 to promote relations with visitors to Palermo and to offer them assistance where needed

Areas Britain: throughout Britain

Italy: Palermo

Ages 18-25

Stay 1/2 weeks, all year

Level of language required None necessary

Activities Guests are invited to join trips to places of interest in Sicily

Accommodation Full board; single/shared bedrooms

Costs Participants pay travel costs only

Travel Host families will meet guests at station or airport

Insurance Not provided

Other services Arrange cultural activities, a welcoming service for families, and help to find suitable partners for groups wishing to arrange their own exchange

NORTHERN IRELAND: FRANCE/FEDERAL REPUBLIC OF GERMANY/SPAIN

Organisation Central Bureau

Address 16 Malone Road, Belfast BT9 5BN Tel 0232-664418/9

Profile Established in 1948 by the British government to act as the national information office and coordinating unit for every type of educational visit exchange. The Northern Ireland office opened in 1980.

Areas France: Angouleme, Poitiers

Germany: Bavaria   Spain: Madrid

Matching Applicants are matched taking age, interests, hobbies and family background into account

Ages 14-19

Stay 3 weeks, July and August

Level of language required Basic knowledge

Activities Host families arrange 2-3 outings per week to places of interest for those visiting Northern Ireland

Accommodation Full board; single/shared bedrooms

Costs Approx £250 inclusive of travel and insurance

Travel Accompanied coach travel for France, air travel for Germany provided; visitors to/from Spain make their own arrangements

Insurance Provided for exchanges with France and Germany

Representation France: Visites et Echanges Culturels et Sportifs Internationaux, 10 rue Ludovic Trarieux, BP295, 16007 Angouleme Tel 95 73 57

Germany: Bayerischer Jugendring, Herzog-Heinrich-Strasse 7, Postfach 20 06 33, 8000 Munich 2 Tel 089 53 05 13

Spain: Ministerio de la Cultura, Instituto de la Juventud, Jose Ortega y Gasset 71, Madrid

Other services Homestays, term time stays, school and class links, teacher exchanges, in-service training courses, and study and hospitality visits

Additional information Open to Northern Ireland residents only

H depending on availability

SCOTLAND: FRANCE/FEDERAL REPUBLIC OF GERMANY

Organisation The Central Bureau

Address 3 Bruntsfield Crescent, Edinburgh EH10 4HD Tel 031-447 8024

Profile Established in 1948 by the British government to act as the national information office and coordinating unit for every type of educational visit and exchange. The Scottish office opened in 1972.

Areas Scotland: Edinburgh

France: Poitou-Charentes region

Germany: Bavaria

Matching Applicants are matched taking age, interests, hobbies and family background into account

Ages Scotland/France: 14-18; Scotland/Germany: 15-18

Stay 3 weeks, July and August

Level of language required 2 years French/school study of German/English

Activities Family outings

Costs Scotland/France: £125 inclusive of full board, escorted coach travel Edinburgh/Angouleme, and insurance. Scotland/Germany: £150 inclusive of full board, escorted rail travel Edinburgh/London, air travel London/Munich and insurance

Travel Families are responsible for travel expenses for their child and the partner between home and departure point

Insurance Provided

Representation France: Visites et Echanges Culturels et Sportifs Internationaux, 10 rue Ludovic-Trarieux, BP295, 16007 Angouleme.

Germany: Bayerischer Jugendring, Herzog-Heinrich-Strasse 7, Postfach 20 06 33, 8000 Munich 2

Other services Homestays, term-time stays, school and class links, teacher exchanges, in-service training courses, and study and hospitality visits

Additional information Scottish/French/German applicants only; apply by beginning March

BRITAIN: SPAIN

Organisation Club de Relaciones Culturales Internacionales

Address Calle Ferraz 82, 28008 Madrid, Spain Tel 479 63 03

Profile A non-profitmaking organisation set up in 1978 to promote cultural, educational and linguistic activities for young people

Areas Throughout Britain and Spain, except Catalonia

Matching Applicants complete a detailed form to enable suitable matching of personal characteristics, family, school, extra-curricula activities, hobbies and special interests

Ages 10-21

Stay 2-4 weeks, Easter, summer and Christmas holidays

Level of language required no knowledge required

Activities Excursions and events arranged

Accommodation Full board; single/shared bedrooms

Costs £25 registration fee plus travel costs

Travel Escorted travel provided for groups; individuals met at airports

Insurance Not included, but advice can be given

Other services Au pair stays, language courses, cultural language trips, and term stays

Additional information A medical certificate and a teacher's reference must be supplied

BRITAIN: UNITED STATES

Organisation Council on International Educational Exchange

Address Seymour Mews House, Seymour Mews, London W1H 9PE Tel 01-935 5594

Profile A non-profitmaking organisation established in 1947 to develop, serve and support international educational exchange as a means to build understanding between nations. The UK/US School Exchange Scheme was set up in 1969 to establish links between secondary schools and to organise exchange visits.

Areas Throughout the United States and Britain

Matching According to ages and interests

Ages Any secondary school age

Stay 4 weeks, March-April, June-July or October-November

Activities Each school arranges its own programme; 3 day stays in London/New York arranged at extra cost

Accommodation Full board with host family; single/shared bedrooms

Costs £385 per pupil inclusive of travel; teacher travels free if 10 pupils in group

Travel Groups are escorted by their teacher; CIEE is on hand at airports

Insurance Provided

Representation CIEE, East 42nd Street, New York, NY 10017, US Tel 212 661 1414

Additional information Schools may organise exchanges by bringing together pupils interested solely in experiencing an American/British way of life, or on the basis of a shared subject interest, allowing the group to pursue particular studies during the exchange, or they may exchange groups such as orchestras or sports teams. Apply 5-10 months before desired date of exchange.

Other services Work exchange programmes

H

BRITAIN: FRANCE/FEDERAL REPUBLIC OF GERMANY/SPAIN/UNITED STATES

Organisation Dragons International

Address The Old Vicarage, South Newington, Banbury, Oxfordshire OX15 4JN Tel Banbury 721717

Profile A commercial organisation founded in 1975, enabling young people to live as a member of a family abroad on a homestay or exchange basis

Areas Throughout Britain, France, Federal Republic of Germany and Spain; eastern seaboard of United States, between Boston and Washington

Matching Applicants are carefully matched with partner of their own age, interests and home background

Ages 11-19

Stay Britain, France and Germany: 2/3 weeks, April, July, August. Spain: 2 weeks, April, July-August. US: 3 weeks, July-August

Level of language required Basic knowledge

Activities Host families arrange outings

Accommodation Full board in single/shared bedrooms

Costs Britain, France and Germany: £99-£144 depending on point of departure, covers return travel, administrative costs and insurance. Spain and US: introduction fee of £60, returned if a suitable partner is not found

Travel Britain: France/Germany: fully supervised coach transport from 13 points in Britain, 12 points France and Germany.
Britain: Spain/US: families make their own travel arrangements. Host families collect guests from arrival point

Insurance Personal liability insurance provided

Representation France: Dragons International, 4 rue de Port Marly, 78750 Mareil-Marly Tel 39 16 54 13

Germany: Dragons International, Sprodentalstrasse 96, 4150 Krefeld Tel 2151 631246

Spain: Dragons International, Buenavista 12, Santo Domingo, Algete (Madrid) Tel 1622 1188

US: Dragons International, 1751 Meriden Road, Wolcott 06716, Connecticut Tel 203 879 9154

FIOCES

SCOTLAND: CANADA/UNITED STATES

Organisation The English Speaking Union of the Commonwealth

Address 22 Atholl Crescent, Edinburgh EH3 8HQ Tel 031-229 1528

Profile An independent voluntary organisation of charitable status founded in 1918, aiming to promote international cooperation and friendship between the peoples of the Commonwealth and the United States by the interchange of persons, knowledge and ideas, and to further understanding and friendship with other countries where this can be made more complete by the use of English as a shared language.

Areas Throughout Scotland, Canada and the United States

Matching Students are placed with families of similar interests

Ages 15-18

Stay 3 weeks, May/June

Activities Students are involved in the everyday life of the families with whom they are staying, they attend high school and take part in a variety of other activities

Accommodation Full board in single/shared bedrooms

Costs £560 travel expenses, plus £7 membership fee

Travel Groups travel with an adult leader

Insurance Provided

Other services Individual work exchange programmes for adult specialists

Additional information Applicants must be recommended by their headteacher and should be involved in the work of their community; British applicants must be attending a Scottish school

H specialist exchange programmes organised

BRITAIN: FRANCE/SPAIN

Organisation Families in Britain

Address Martins Cottage, Martins Lane, Birdham, Chichester, Sussex PO20 7AU Tel Chichester 512222

Profile A commercial company founded in 1960 specialising in introducing overseas visitors to private families

Areas Throughout Britain, France and Spain

Matching Applicants are carefully selected by matching ages, interests, hobbies and background

Ages 14-18

Stay Throughout the year

Activities Host families organise visits to local places of interest

Costs Agency fee approx £60

Travel Visitors can be met at air/sea ports

Insurance Not provided

Other services Sports and special interest courses

Representation Germany: S&H Deyerlei, Eichhornchenweg 3, 2080 Pinneberg Tel 04101/61744 (10.00-20.00 hours)

Spain: Petrina Murray, Residencial Horizonte No 30 (3o, 1o), Majadahonda, Madrid Tel 91-638-7334

Additional information Apply at least 2 months in advance

H depending on disability

BRITAIN: FRANCE/FEDERAL REPUBLIC OF GERMANY

Organisation Gesellschaft fur Internationale Jugendkontakte eV

Address Am Helpert 32-34, Postfach 200 562, 5300 Bonn 2, Federal Republic of Germany Tel 32 26 49

Profile A non-profitmaking organisation founded in 1983, arranging homestays and exchanges

Areas Throughout Britain, France and the Federal Republic

Matching Participants are carefully matched according to background, hobbies, interests and location

Ages 13-18

Stay 2-3 weeks, all year

Level of language required Fair knowledge of the host language preferable

Activities Families arrange outings

Accommodation Full board with host families

Costs Administration fee plus travel costs

Travel Escorted travel by coach arranged

Insurance Not provided

Other services Homestays, au pair placements and guides on work opportunities for young people

BRITAIN: FRANCE/FEDERAL REPUBLIC OF GERMANY

Organisation Interspeak Ltd

Address 14 Robin Hill Drive, Standish, near Wigan, Greater Manchester WN6 0QW Tel Standish 421960

Profile A commercial organisation founded in 1981 to provide good family accommodation for foreign students and to improve international relationships among young people

Areas Britain: Blackpool, Southport, Manchester, York and London France: Poitiers, Angouleme   Germany: Frankfurt area, individuals/small groups; Munich, groups of 20+

Matching Applicants should have similar interests, hobbies and ages; great care is taken to ensure a good match between students

Ages Britain/France: 13-18; Britain/Germany: 14-20

Stay 2-3 weeks; July and August, and Easter (France only)

Level of language required Basic knowledge of English helpful for exchanges to Britain

Activities Family outings; organised activities sometimes available

Accommodation Single bedrooms

Costs Britain/France: £115-£125; Britain/Germany:£179. Costs include full board, escorted travel, insurance and administrative costs.

Travel Britain/France: in groups by coach via London, Calais and Paris. Britain/Germany: in groups by air, London to Frankfurt/Munich. Large groups are escorted; representative at departure/arrival points.

Insurance Personal liability cover provided

Other services Homestays, language holidays

Representation France: VECSI, 10 rue Ludovic Trarieux, 16007 Angouleme Tel 95 73 57

Germany: Herr G Welti, Realschulrektur, Staatliche Realschule, Luitpold-Baumann-Strasse 37, 8716 Dettelbach Tel 093 24 693/ Bayerischer Jugendring, Herzog-Heinrich-Strasse 7, Postfach 200603, 8000 Munchen 2 Tel 089 53 05 13

Additional information Britain/France exchange participants choose whether to visit or receive first. German partners usually travel back immediately with the English participants to complete the exchange.

H accepted

BRITAIN: AUSTRIA

Organisation Osterreichische Vereinigung fur Austausch und Studienreisen (OVAST)

Address Dr Gschmeidlerstrasse 10/4, 3500 Krems, PO Box 148, Austria Tel 02732 5743

Profile A non-profitmaking organisation founded in 1964 arranging homestays and exchanges

Areas Throughout Britain and Austria

Matching Partners are matched according to age, hobbies and interests

Ages Mainly 10-20; school groups 14-17

Stay 2-3 weeks July-August for individuals; 3-6 weeks all year for school groups

Level of language required none for individuals; some knowledge for school groups

Activities Host families are encouraged to arrange outings. Participants in school exchanges attend various schools and take part in school activities; also sightseeing and visits to the theatre at extra cost.

Accommodation Full board in selected families

Costs Individuals: AS4788 plus AS550 administration fee; groups: AS9285 for the first 3 weeks plus AS1733 for each additional week

Travel Escorted travel by train provided

Insurance Provided

Other services Homestays, skiing holidays

FIYTO FIOCES

BRITAIN: FRANCE/FEDERAL REPUBLIC OF GERMANY/SPAIN

Organisation The Robertson Organisation

Address 44 Willoughby Road, London NW3 1RU Tel 01-435 4907

Profile A private organisation founded in 1948 to promote language learning and understanding among young people of Europe

Areas Britain: throughout England, Scotland and Wales

France: Paris and surrounding area, Lyon

Germany: Cologne, Dusseldorf and surrounding areas

Spain: northern Spain

Matching Experience and expertise is used to match those who it is felt have a real chance of getting on well together. Prefer to meet applicants and parents; appointments can be booked.

Ages 11-21

Stay 2-3 weeks, Christmas, Easter and July/August, depending on country

Level of language required 1 year, preferably

Language tuition Not provided

Activities Families arrange outings on a reciprocal basis

Accommodation Full board in carefully selected families; single/twin bedrooms

Costs £112 inclusive of return travel ex London

Travel Participants travel in escorted groups and are met by host families at the destination. Escorted travel from Paris to destination provided where necessary.

Insurance Can be arranged

Representation France: L'Organisation Robertson, 51 rue de la Harpe, 75005 Paris Tel 46 33 12 89

Additional information Provide guidelines on how to prepare for an exchange.

H depending on nature of handicap

FIOCES

BRITAIN: BELGIUM

Organisation Service de la Jeunesse de la Province de Liege

Address rue Belvaux 123, 4030 Grivegnee (Liege), Belgium Tel 422600/437402

Profile A public organisation aiming to give young people the opportunity to travel at low cost and to learn about the economic, cultural and linguistic background of foreign countries

Areas Throughout Britain and the province of Liege, Belgium

Ages 15-19

Stay 10-15 days, July or August

Level of language required Basic knowledge helpful

Activities Optional cultural, sporting and social activities and excursions arranged

Accommodation Full board with the host family

Costs Participants pay travel costs only

Travel Escorted group travel by cheapest means

Insurance Provided

Other services A wide range of courses for young people, and operate youth, documentation and information centres

Additional information Preparatory meetings arranged for participants and their families; a representative of the Service is available throughout the stay

TERM STAYS

BRITAIN: UNITED STATES

Organisation American Institute for Foreign Study Scholarship Foundation

Address 37 Queen's Gate, London SW7 5HR Tel 01-581 2733

Profile The American Institute for Foreign Study was founded in 1964 to provide study and travel programmes for teachers and students interested in learning about other cultures. The AIFS Scholarship Foundation is a non-profitmaking organisation established in 1968 to promote international understanding through cross-cultural exchange.

Areas Throughout the US, and Bromley near London

Ages US: 15-19; Britain: 15-18

Stay US: August-January/June, and January-June; Britain: September-December/June and January-June

Activities Family outings and extra-curricular activities

Accommodation In carefully selected host families; single/shared bedrooms

Costs US: $2095 5 months, $2895 10 months including 3-day orientation programme in New York/San Francisco. Weekday school lunch, return travel and $25 registration fee extra.

Britain: $2250 September-January; $3395 January-June; $4495 academic year. Includes orientation course in New York, tuition, room and board, flight New York-London for students who meet enrolment deadlines, but not school meals

Travel Staff meet students on arrival; help provided on all aspects of US travel

Insurance Health and accident insurance provided

Other services Au pair placements in America

Representation AIFS Scholarship Foundation, 100 Greenwich Avenue, Greenwich, Connecticut 06830, US Tel 203 869 9090

Additional information Applicants must provide school reports for the last 3 years, 2 letters of recommendation from teachers and a health certificate. British participants should apply by 1 April/1 October for programmes beginning January/August. US applications must be postmarked by July 15/October 15 programmes beginning September/January.

H cases considered individually

BRITAIN: CANADA/UNITED STATES

Organisation ASSE International Programme

Address 6 Harcourt Street, London W1H 2BD Tel 01-724 0280 or PO Box 20, Harwich, Essex, CO12 4DQ Tel Harwich 506347

Profile A non-profitmaking organisation established in 1978 under the auspices of the Swedish and Finnish Ministries of Education to increase international understanding between young people. Operates a 1 year high school exchange scheme between Britain and North America.

Areas Throughout Britain, Canada and the United States

Ages 16-18

Stay 10 months, August-June

Activities Students take part in the life of the host family and are enrolled at a local high school; special excursions also organised

Accommodation Host families must supply references and are interviewed before selection; the student is integrated as a full member of the family

Costs £1950 inclusive of full board, travel, insurance, and presence of representative during the stay

Travel Escorted return flight; transfer assistance to host family where necessary

Insurance Comprehensive medical insurance provided

US representation ASSE, 228 North Coast Highway, Laguna Beach, CA 92651

Additional information Information meetings before departure; orientation meeting soon after arrival and area representative meetings arranged throughout the stay. Applicants must provide good character and academic references, and demonstrate potential to benefit from the experience of the exchange. Apply by the end of the year; matching commences in January.

H where possible

BRITAIN: FRANCE

Organisation Association pour les Voyages Educatifs (AVE)/Maison de Cambridge

Address 1 rue General Riu, 34000 Montpellier, France Tel 67 64 07 86

Profile A non-profitmaking voluntary organisation, AVE is an educational visit/exchange organisation founded in 1984; Maison de Cambridge, founded in 1978 as the Centre Britanique, is a British cultural centre set up in 1985 by members of the local education authorities in Montpellier and Cambridge as part of Community Link.

Areas France: Languedoc-Roussillon region

Britain: Cambridge, Aberdeenshire, Northern Ireland and other areas

Ages 11-18

Stay 1+ months, all year

Level of language required Minimum 2 years study

Activities Participants stay with a family and attend a private school

Accommodation Single/shared bedrooms in family home

Costs £60-65 administrative fee, travel extra; board/lodging not charged on exchanges, and schools do not tend to charge fees

Travel Advice given; participants are met on arrival by host families

Insurance Not included

Other services Exchanges, homestays, au pair placements and working holidays

British representation Community Education Department, Shire Hall, Cambridge/Alliance Francaise, 29 Barton Road, Newnham, Cambridge/ Montpellier Exchange Register, Rainey Endowed School, Magherafelt, Northern Ireland

Additional information To ensure that visiting children do not speak too much of their own language, no extra courses or activities are arranged

H accepted

NORTHERN IRELAND: FEDERAL REPUBLIC OF GERMANY

Organisation The Central Bureau

Address 16 Malone Road, Belfast BT9 5BN Tel 0232-664418/9

Profile Established in 1948 by the British government to act as the national information office and coordinating unit for every type of educational visit. The Northern Ireland office opened in 1980.

Areas Bavaria, and throughout Northern Ireland

Ages 16-18

Stay 1 term, autumn, spring or summer

Level of language required Students should be studying the language to A level or equivalent

Activities Participants stay with a family and attend a local state school; families are expected to arrange outings

Accommodation Single/shared bedrooms in family home

Costs Stays are on a reciprocal or paying guest basis. On reciprocal exchanges no charge is made for board and lodging; paying guests pay £60 per week. All participants pay their own travel costs.

Travel Participants make their own arrangements

Insurance Not included

Other services Exchanges, school and class links, in-service training courses, and study and hospitality visits

Representation Bayerischer Jugendring, Herzog-Heinrich-Strasse 7, Postfach 20 06 33, 8000 Munich 2 Tel 089 53 035 13

Additional information Open to Northern Ireland/German residents only. On reciprocal exchanges applicants are matched taking age, interests, hobbies and family background into account.

H depending on availability

SCOTLAND: FEDERAL REPUBLIC OF GERMANY

Organisation The Central Bureau

Address 3 Bruntsfield Crescent, Edinburgh EH10 4HD Tel 031-447 8024

Profile Established in 1948 by the British government to act as the national information office and coordinating unit for every type of educational visit and exchange. The Scottish office opened in 1972.

Areas Bavaria, Schleswig-Holstein, and throughout Scotland

Ages 16-17, and those between school and university

Stay 12-14 weeks, autumn or spring term

Level of language required Good knowledge necessary

Activities Participants are placed with a family and attend a local school; no extra activities arranged

Costs Board and lodging: DM100 per week, Germany; £30 per week, Scotland. Central Bureau may be able to provide bursaries for Scottish participants; German government may provide up to DM50 towards expenses.

Travel Participants travel individually; help and advice offered

Insurance Full health insurance arranged

Representation Bayrischer Jugendring, Herzog-Heinrich-Strasse 7, Postfach 20 06 33, 8000 Munich 2, Federal Republic of Germany

Other services Homestays, exchanges, school and class links, in-service training courses, and study and hospitality visits

Additional information Participants should be recommended by their schools. Scottish/German applicants only; apply by end September for spring visits/end April for autumn visits.

H accepted

BRITAIN: SPAIN

Organisation Club de Relaciones Culturales Internacionales

Address Calle Ferraz 82, 28008 Madrid, Spain Tel 479 63 03

Profile A non-profitmaking organisation set up in 1978 to promote cultural, educational and linguistic activities for young people

Areas Throughout Spain except Catalonia

Ages 10-21

Stay 1+ terms or full academic year

Level of language required No knowledge necessary

Language tuition Spanish tuition included in regular school programme

Activities Participants are placed in local state or private schools and take part in school activities; excursions and events also arranged

Accommodation Full board in family homes; single/shared bedrooms

Costs Registration fee £40 plus travel costs; as this is a reciprocal scheme no other costs should be involved

Travel Escorted travel provided for groups; individuals met at airports

Insurance Not included but advice can be given

Other services Exchanges, au pair stays and language courses

Additional information Applicants complete a detailed form to enable suitable matching of personal characteristics, family, school, extra-curricula activities, hobbies and special interests; medical certificate and teacher's reference must be supplied.

BRITAIN: FRANCE/UNITED STATES

Organisation Educational Foundation for Foreign Study

Address EF Educational Services, EF House, 1 Farman Street, Hove, Brighton, Sussex BN3 1AL Tel Brighton 723651

Profile EF is a commercial organisation set up in 1965, specialising in educational travel and language schools. The EF Foundation is a non-profitmaking, non-political organisation founded in 1979, committed to promoting international understanding through language education and cultural exchange. The US school year is designated by the US government as an official exchange visitor programme.

Areas Throughout Britain, France, United States

Ages 14-18

Stay 10 months/1 academic year, departing July/August; 6 months programme available in France

Level of language required At least 2 years study

Activities Participants attend local maintained school full time; school and family activities

Accommodation With carefully selected host families; single/shared bedrooms

Costs Britain: varies, depending on exchange rate; France: £1,745; US: £1,965. Costs include travel, board and lodging, preparation material, information meetings, school tuition, and local representative services

Travel Escorted group return travel and transfers included

Insurance Not included

Other services Language courses, high school year in Europe

US representation EF, 1528 Chapala Street, Santa Barbara, CA 93101 Tel 805-963-0553/EF, 235 Greenwich Avenue, Greenwich, CT 06830 Tel 203-629-2754

Additional information Optional 2-3 week preparation course on arrival, tours and excursions available. Applicants should have a satisfactory academic standard and must have a letter of recommendation from a teacher. Interviews take place September-March. Area representatives select host families and schools and keep in contact with participants during the year.

H cases considered individually

BRITAIN: FRANCE

Organisation En Famille

Address Jerusalem House, Orchard Terrace, Totnes, Devon TQ9 5EY
Tel Totnes 866120

Profile A non-profitmaking organisation founded in 1978, registered in
France as a charity and run by volunteers. Aims to give English and
French children the opportunity to acquaint themselves, in depth, with
each other's language and culture.

Areas Mainly in NW France and SW England; some contacts in other
parts of both countries

Matching Careful preparation is involved in the matching of families,
and applicants are personally visited

Ages 8-11

Stay 6 months; the child will usually begin to speak the other language
fluently by 3 months

Level of language required Basic knowledge helpful

Activities The visiting child is treated as a member of the family and
takes part in family activities

Accommodation Full board

Costs £200 inclusive of host school fee, travelling expenses and
administration costs

Travel Help is given with arrangements for visits and transfer of
children to host families

Insurance Not provided

Representation Jacques & Katherine Pinault, 14 rue Perronet, 61000
Alencon, France Tel 33 29 59 44

Additional information Permission must be obtained from the schools
for the visiting child to attend lessons. Families may make preliminary
visits. Ideally, information about prospective participants should be
received 2/3 years in advance so that the exchange can be thoroughly
prepared.

H depending on circumstances

ENGLAND, WALES, IRELAND & CHANNEL ISLANDS

Organisation European Educational Opportunities Programme

Address 28 Canterbury Road, Lydden, Dover, Kent CT15 7ER Tel Dover 823631

Profile A non-profitmaking organisation founded in 1986 aiming to offer high-quality programmes through carefully selected homes, schools and allied agencies

Areas Surrey, Kent, Essex, East Anglia, West Country, Channel Islands, Wales and Ireland

Ages 16+

Stay 1+ terms, all year

Level of English required Basic knowledge desirable

Language tuition Private English tuition arranged on request

Activities Participants attend local grammar/high schools and enter fully into academic and social programmes

Accommodation Students are totally integrated into the family

Costs £250 per month full board, plus £10 registration fee

Travel Participants are met at port of arrival

Insurance Not provided

Other services Homestays, class visits, city adventure and work experience programmes

Representation France: ANEAS, 54 Grande Rue, 89113 Fleury la Vallee

Germany: Jeuneurope-Studienfahrten, Oststrasse 162, 4000 Dusseldorf 1

Additional information Participants must be recommended by their school. Students are supported and supervised by a member of staff; parents may telephone at any time to discuss problems or areas of concern.

ENGLAND

Organisation Eurolanguage Ltd

Address Greyhound House, 23/24 George Street, Richmond, Surrey TW9 1HY Tel 01-940 1087/948 5846

Profile A commercial organisation founded in 1972, concerned with the promotion of English life, culture and language

Areas In selected independent boarding schools throughout England

Ages 13+, but mainly sixth formers

Stay September-July; students may also start in the spring term

Level of English required Adequate knowledge of English necessary

Language tuition Extra language classes available, and may be necessary at first

Activities Students can take part in all school activities; they can opt to be weekly boarders and spend the weekend with families who may arrange other activities

Accommodation In single/shared dormitories during the term, and with a family during holidays and possibly weekends

Costs Variable, depending on the school

Travel Arrangements are made for the family to meet students at the airport

Insurance Not provided

Other services Homestays, English language and sports courses, short study and tailor-made tours

Additional information There is usually an orientation period spent with family before the student starts school

H accepted, depending on school

UNITED STATES

Organisation The Experiment in International Living

Address Otesaga, West Malvern Road, Upper Wyche, Malvern, Worcestershire, WR14 4EN Tel Malvern 62577

Profile A non-profitmaking educational travel organisation founded in 1936, Offering students the opportunity to live with an American family and to study in high school

Areas Cities, small towns and rural areas throughout the US

Ages 16-19

Stay Semester programme: 5 months, starting August or January; academic year programme: 10 months, starting August

Level of English required Minimum 3 years study together with comprehensive written/oral knowledge

Activities Students are enrolled in a local high school where they participate in course work and extra-curricular activities, and are often invited to help in language and other classes

Accommodation Full board in a family

Costs Semester programme £1,500, academic year programme £1,910, dependent on exchange rates; includes travel within, but not to, the US

Travel Escorted group travel to the US; students are met on arrival by host families

Insurance Included

Other services Special interest programmes, homestays and au pair placements

Overseas representation Over 45 offices worldwide: details from UK office

Additional information Apply by 15 March for August programmes, 15 October for January programme. Early application advised; places are very limited. Students are selected for their ability to adjust to another culture, family, and school environment.

H with advance notification

WORLDWIDE

Organisation International Educational Programmes

Address Seymour Mews House, Seymour Mews, London W1H 9PE Tel 01-486 5462

Profile A registered charity founded in 1947, working towards peace through international understanding by promoting relationships in which people from differing cultural background share new learning situations

Areas Europe, Egypt, Jordan, United States, Mexico, Venezuela, Brazil and most Latin American countries, Hong Kong, Indonesia, Japan, Australia

Ages 16-18

Stay 11 months from July/August or from January/February. Participants visiting Peru, Brazil and Australia and who have a confirmed university place may return in late September.

Level of language required Varies

Language tuition Short introductory course provided on arrival

Activities Participants attend school full-time and become a member of the community. Group activities, language and cultural orientation courses organised; host families may arrange outings.

Accommodation Applicants are carefully placed with a family and in a community which complements their background

Costs From £700-£2700, includes travel, full board, pocket money, medical expenses, orientation courses, group activities, school and family placement, and support and supervision throughout the stay. Parents are asked to make a realistic contribution which is within their means; participants will be encouraged to seek grants from local trusts and companies.

Travel Included

Insurance Included

Representation AFS International/Intercultural Programmes, 313 East 43rd Street, New York, NY 10017, United States

Additional information Applicants must be attending school full time, in good health, adaptable and willing to give a lot to the experience

ENGLAND

Organisation Language & Leisure Services

Address 228A High Street, Bromley, Kent BR1 1PQ Tel 01-460 4861
Profile A private organisation founded in 1959 to enable and
encourage young people from overseas to come to England at realistic
cost and to learn about England, its way of life, language and culture

Areas At various independent boarding schools in countryside districts
throughout England

Ages Approx 12-17

Stay 1+ terms; also 3-5 week stays towards the end of the summer
term

Level of English required Minimum intermediate level

Language tuition Schools will arrange extra English classes if
necessary

Activities Students can take part in all school activities

Accommodation In single/shared school dormitories; all holiday
periods are spent at home

Costs Vary, depending on school; approx £100 per week for short
stays, approx £1000-£1500 per term for termstays. Travel not included.

Escorted travel Can be arranged

Insurance Not provided

Other services Homestays, English language summer courses and
study tours

PRACTICAL INFORMATION

Preparation In all probability, once you have been matched with a suitable family or exchange partner you will be required to write to them and introduce yourself. The more contact there is between the families concerned in an exchange, and to some extent a homestay, the easier and more successful the experience will be. Although much of the information here is written from the point of view of helping parents with a child going on a homestay or exchange, it is equally valid to older participants. Preliminary correspondence is important in learning about the family, the basic social behaviour and the food, for example, in the home to be visited, and goes a long way in helping to minimise culture shocks and homesickness that can often be experienced when there has been little opportunity to learn about the customs and social conventions observed. Particularly in the case of an exchange of school pupils the first letters could be in the foreign language, and the children's teachers will probably help if there are any difficulties. Tell your exchange partner about yourself, your family, pets, interests and hobbies, and it's a good idea to send photographs of you, your family and your home. If you write in your native language make sure that your letters are grammatically correct, and that all return correspondence is promptly answered. If it is necessary to telephone the host family to check on arrangements try to arrange it so that someone is on hand who speaks the language well or that you have rehearsed what you wish to say. If you or the child have any doubts or worries about going abroad once the homestay or exchange has been set up, try to talk the problems through. Encourage the child to talk to his/her language teacher or to other

children who have been on a homestay or exchange visit. Full preparation for the experience of foreign travel and the different way of life to be encountered is vital if the visit is to be beneficial. It is particularly important for parents to try to teach their children tolerance and the ability to see another's point of view. Try to find out as much as possible about the country you are visiting. Visit your local library and see what books and other information they hold on the country to be visited. The appropriate tourist office should be able to provide maps and general information of the country and the specific area in which you will be staying, and the embassy may also be able to provide information; see Contact Addresses. If you are staying abroad for a particularly long time or on a term stay, it is wise to pay a visit to your doctor and dentist before you go, to reduce any likelihood of your falling ill during your stay. Further details of medical preparation are given under Health Requirements.

What to take with you Don't take more than you can comfortably carry, especially if you are planning to bring souvenirs and presents back with you. Do not pack your passport, tickets and money in your suitcase, but keep them within easy reach in your hand luggage. You would be well advised not to take anything valuable, but if you must, make sure you have it in sight at all times. It might be a nice gesture to take along a small present for your exchange partner or host family, perhaps something typical of your country or local area. You could also take pictures and information about your home area, as these would be of interest to your partner, especially if they are coming to visit you.
The following checklist may prove helpful:

Passport
Pocket money
Camera and film(s)
Tourist information
Notebook and pens
Phrase book
Address book
Sportswear
Swimming costume
Sun protection items
Comfortable shoes and clothes
Smart clothes for special occasions
Information about your area
Prescribed medicines
Form E111
Small gift

Pocket money The amount of money you take with you on the stay will depend very much on the services already covered by the cost. Those opting for homestays with half board, for example, should remember to take enough money to cover the cost of the remaining meal each day. In addition you may need money to pay for entrance fees at museums, art galleries for example, although occasionally such things will be paid for by the host family. In some cases an allowance may have been made to them to cover extra expenditure such as outings, but this is not always so, and it is as well to check beforehand with the organisation so that any possible embarrassment or uncertainty is avoided. Remember that the cost of living in the country you are visiting may be higher than you are used to. Organisations should be able to advise on how much money to take as pocket money and to cover expenses. It is advisable for any visitor to a foreign country to have a sufficient supply of money, preferably in travellers' cheques, to cover unforeseen circumstances. A good guide is to make sure that you take enough to pay for one or two nights' hotel accommodation and a long-distance telephone call. If you do run out of money, try to phone your parents to explain the situation; it is possible to arrange for money to be transferred to a bank abroad. In a dire emergency, your embassy or consulate in the country you are visiting will be able to advise on funds, or pay for your travel home if there is no other source of finance available.

Passports A UK passport costs £15 (£22.50 if particulars of family are included) and is valid for 10 years. A 94 page passport, useful for those intending to travel through many countries, is available at a cost of £30. Both are obtainable from regional offices:

Passport Office, Clive House, 70-78 Petty France, London SW1H 9HD Tel 01-213 3434

Passport Office, 5th Floor, India Buildings, Water Street, Liverpool L2 0QZ Tel 051-237 3010

Passport Office, Olympia House, Upper Dock Street, Newport, Gwent NPT 1XA Tel Newport 56292

Passport Office, 55 Westfield Road, Peterborough, Cambridgeshire PE3 6TG Tel Peterborough 895555

Passport Office, 1st Floor, Empire House, 131 West Nile Street, Glasgow G1 2RY Tel 041-332 0271

Passport Office, Hampton House, 47-53 High Street, Belfast BT1 2QS Tel 0232-232371

Application forms are available from main post offices. The completed form should be sent or taken to the area passport office. Processing the application takes at least four weeks and can take even longer during the summer months.

Within western Europe (excluding the German Democratic Republic and East Berlin) and certain other specified countries, you can travel on a British Visitor's Passport. This costs £7.50 (£11.25 if particulars of family are included) but is valid only for 12 months. Application forms are obtainable from any main post office, Monday-Friday and should be returned there; in most cases the Passport will be issued immediately. Applicants from Northern Ireland, Jersey, Guernsey and the Isle of Man must call at the relevant area passport office. The British Visitor's Passport can be issued to British citizens, British Dependent Territories Citizens and British Overseas citizens for holiday purposes of up to three months. *Essential Information for Holders of UK Passports who Intend to Travel Overseas*, a booklet containing notes on illness or injury while abroad, insurance, vaccinations, NHS medical cards (for those going abroad for more than 3 months), consular assistance overseas, British Customs and other useful advice, is available from all passport offices. If a passport is lost or stolen while abroad, the local police should be notified immediately. If necessary the nearest British Embassy or Consulate will issue a substitute. It is wise to keep a separate note of the passport number.

Visas For entry to some countries, especially in Eastern Europe, a visa or visitor's pass is required, and in many countries a residence permit will be required. Organisations arranging stays in such countries will be able to advise, and details of application procedures are available from the consular section of the appropriate embassy. Regulations are subject to change without warning, and you are advised to obtain precise information before setting out.

Identity cards The International Student/Scholar Identity Card (ISIC) scheme is operated by the International Student Travel Conference, a group of major official student travel bodies worldwide, promoting special travel and other discount benefits for students. The Card provides internationally accepted proof of the bona fide status of students and consequently ensures that they may enjoy many special facilities, including fare reductions, cheap accommodation, reduced rates or free entry to museums, art galleries and historic sites. It is obtainable from officially appointed local student travel offices, and available to scholars aged 16/22 and all full-time students, regardless of nationality, at a cost of £3.50 inclusive of the International Student Travel Guide detailing the International Discount Scheme and facilities worldwide. It is valid for a maximum of 15 months (1 October-31 December of the following year) and must be renewed annually.

The FIYTO Youth International Educational Exchange Card is an internationally recognised identity card offering concessions to young travellers including transport, accommodation, restaurants, excursions, cultural events and reduced rates or free entry to many museums, art galleries, theatres and cinemas. Available to all those under 26 it costs £3 inclusive of an annual booklet giving details of concessions available. FIYTO Cards are available in Britain from all STA Travel Offices.

Health requirements Changes in food and climate may cause minor illnesses, and, especially when visiting hot countries, it is wise to take extra care in your hygiene, eating and drinking habits. If you do visit a hot country you should never underestimate the strength of the sun, or overestimate your own strength. Drink plenty of fluid, make sure there is enough salt in your diet, wear loose-fitting cotton clothes, even a hat, take things easy and watch out for heat exhaustion, heat stroke and sunburn. This advice may seem over-cautious, but it would be a shame to let the climate spoil your holiday. The Department of Health and Social Security publishes a leaflet *SA35 Protect Your Health Abroad* which includes vital information for people travelling overseas, especially to hotter climates. It contains information on vaccinations, precautions to be taken with regard to health while abroad, and what to do in case of an emergency. Available from the Department of Health and Social Security, International Relations (Health), Alexander Fleming House, Elephant and Castle, London SE1 6BY Tel 01-407 5522 ext 6749. If you are taking prescribed drugs you are strongly advised to carry a doctor's letter giving details of the medical condition and the medication, avoiding the possibility of confusion. A certificate of vaccination against certain diseases is an entry requirement for some countries. It is wise to consult embassies on this point, since such requirements are continually subject to review; alternatively, contact the Department of Health and Social Security.

Health insurance A person is only covered by the NHS while in the UK, and will usually have to pay the full costs of any treatment abroad themself. However, there are health care arrangements with all the European Community (EC) countries (Belgium, Denmark, France, Federal Republic of Germany, Greece, Ireland, Italy, Luxembourg, Netherlands, Portugal and Spain.) In most of them free or reduced cost emergency treatment for visitors is provided only on production of form *E111*. Leaflet

SA30, Medical Costs Abroad, available from local offices of the Department of Health and Social Security, explains who is covered by the arrangements and how to apply for form *E111*. It includes a list of all the countries where free or reduced cost medical treatment is available, together with details of what treatment is free or at reduced cost in EC countries, and gives the procedures which must be followed to get treatment in countries where form *E111* is not needed (usually Denmark and Ireland); travellers are advised to get the leaflet well before they leave the UK. Form *E111* is issued with an information sheet on how to get emergency medical treatment in other EC countries. Form *E111* or leaflet *SA30* must be taken abroad and, if emergency treatment is needed, the correct procedures must be followed. In addition, there are reciprocal health care arrangements with Australia, Austria, Bulgaria, Channel Islands, Czechoslovakia, Finland, German Democratic Republic, Gibraltar, Hong Kong, Hungary, Iceland, Isle of Man, Malta, New Zealand, Norway, Poland, Romania, Sweden, USSR, Yugoslavia and British Dependent Territories of Anguilla, British Virgin Islands, Falkland Islands, Montserrat, St Helena, and Turks and Caicos Islands. However, private health insurance may still be needed in these countries; leaflet *SA30* should be read to check the services available. If a person is going away for more than 3 months they should hand their NHS medical card to the immigration officer at their port of departure, or send it to their local Family Practitioner Committee (England and Wales), Area Health Board (Scotland) or Central Services Agency (Northern Ireland), with a note of their date of departure. If they have lost or mislaid their card they should write to the same address (see local telephone directory), giving date of departure, last permanent address in this country, name and address of their doctor, and NHS medical numbers. If, however, they are going to Bulgaria, Poland, Iceland or Hong Kong they may need their NHS medical card to get free treatment, so should not hand it in. See leaflet *SA30* for details. It has not yet been possible to make arrangements for UK passport holders to receive free or subsidised medical treatment in countries other than those previously mentioned; also, the Reciprocal Health Agreements and E111 arrangements cover many eventualities, but the coverage given under each national provision may not always be comprehensive. You may be required to pay for medicines or part of the treatment, and in any case, the cost of flying you home is never included. It is therefore strongly advisable to take out adequate private medical insurance. Full details of health insurance are obtainable from the Department of Health and Social Security, International Relations (Health), Alexander Fleming House, Elephant and Castle, London SE1 6BY Tel 01-407 5522 (ext 6737 for EC enquiries; ext 6824 for other enquiries). Overseas visitors to the UK will be charged the full cost of medical treatment if there are no reciprocal health arrangements between their country and the UK. It is advisable to check what arrangements exist and to take out adequate private medical insurance where necessary.

Travel insurance Many organisations either include insurance cover in their price, or can arrange it at additional cost. It is important to ascertain exactly what is included in the cover offered, as frequently it is limited to third party risk or public liability.

Third party risk only provides cover for persons other than the individual concerned, while public liability concerns injury to people or damage to property, arising specifically from carelessness on the part of the company concerned. It is up to you to decide exactly what extent of insurance cover you require. Remember that certain countries operate a health care agreement with the UK (see Health insurance, but you will almost certainly need some kind of cover for personal possessions, luggage, money and travellers' cheques; and against cancellation, delay, personal accident and personal liability.

The ISIS (International Student Insurance Service) policy provides, at competitive rates, a wide range of benefits covering death, disablement, medical and other personal expenses, loss of luggage, personal liability and cancellation, loss of deposits or curtailment. An advantage of this policy is that medical expenses can be settled on the spot in many countries by student organisations cooperating with ISIS; the medical limit for these expenses relates to each claim and therefore the cover is, in effect, limitless. An English-speaking medical 24 hour emergency assistance service is provided to handle all medical emergencies. Details from Endsleigh Insurance Services Ltd, Endsleigh House, Ambrose Street, Cheltenham Spa, Gloucestershire GL50 3NR Tel Cheltenham 36151 or the local Endsleigh insurance office or student travel centre.

Currency Foreign currency can be obtained before you leave at major travel agents and at bureau de change branches of banks. Other bank branches may need a few days' notice. You can shop around to get the best exchange rate, but remember that commission is charged on the sale of currency. Some local currency is essential, especially if you are due to arrive at the weekend, but travellers cheques are safer than cash, and you also get a better rate of exchange. Sterling travellers' cheques are issued by the clearing banks and will need to be ordered at least a week in advance. You will need to show your passport, and pay charges. Do not countersign the cheques in advance. Make a note of the numbers and keep it separate from the cheques; in this way, if you lose the cheques they can still be replaced. Some travellers' cheques can be replaced while you are still abroad, others will be honoured by the issuing bank on your return. If you are visiting North or South America, US$ travellers' cheques can be used as cash. If you have a current account at a British bank, you will probably be able to obtain a supply of Eurocheques and a cheque card. These cheques can be cashed abroad at banks displaying the Eurocheque sign, and are also accepted by many shops. A small charge may be levied in some countries, and charges may be higher in bureaux de change. The cheques are drawn against your current account and are guaranteed up to an agreed amount, usually equivalent to 300 Swiss Francs. Don't forget to take some of your own currency with you for use on the outward and return journeys.

Travel Some organisations are happy to make or advise on all necessary travel/escort arrangements, although this service is not always included in the price. Other organisations expect individuals to make their own way to a particular point of departure where they will then join a group. The cost of travel to the point of departure would then be the responsibility of the individual. On arrival in the host country, participants are either met by the host families, or make their own way to the town where they will be staying, in some cases at their own cost. For those wishing to make their own arrangements, there are a number of specialist operators and low-cost tickets available for young people. Visitors to Britain are normally met at the point of arrival by a representative of the organisation or by the host family. Where this is not the case, you should make your own way from the port or airport to an arranged meeting place. Both London Heathrow and Gatwick airports are well served by underground trains and buses. On arrival, ask at the information desk for advice. Most major sea ports in the UK are served by good rail and road links with the rest of the country.

By road It is becoming increasingly popular to travel to mainland Europe, and beyond, by coach. The main advantages of this form of transport are that it is cheap, and that you are not required to carry luggage for any great distance since you stay with the same vehicle for the entire journey. A number of operators run this kind of service. Contact International Express Services, National Express, Western House, 237-239 Oxford Street, London W1R 1AB Tel 01-439 9368, or associated agencies for details. Destinations include Belgium, France, Federal Republic of Germany, Greece, Italy, Netherlands, Poland, Portugal, Spain, Sweden, Turkey, Ireland, Channel Islands and the Isle of Man. Bus and coach travel are the cheapest form of public transport within the UK. Coach companies operate express services between major towns. It is sometimes advisable to book your seat in advance. Contact National Travel,

Victoria Coach Station, London SW1W 9TP Tel 01-730 0202 for further details on services throughout the country. For those wishing to travel to Britain by coach, the National Express European representatives are:

Belgium: L'Epervier, 50 place de Bronckere, Brussels Tel 7,0025

France: Eurolines, 8 place Stalingrad, Paris Tel 4205 1210; Francebus, rue Gustave Nadaud, Lyon Tel 7872 3523

Federal Republic of Germany: Bayern Express, Mannheimerstrasse, Berlin Tel 33/34 870511; Deutsche Touring, Romerhof, Frankfurt Tel 79030; Deutsche Touring, Arnulfstrasse 3, Starnberger Bahnhof, Munich 2 Tel 591824

Greece: Xenagos, 3 Stadiou St, Syntagma Square, Athens 152 Tel 2180; Eurolines, Tsimiski 32, Thessaloniki Tel 283268

Ireland: CIE, Busaras Bus Station, Dublin, Tel 787777

Italy: CIT, 64 Plazza Republica, Rome Tel 4794407; Lazzi Express, Piazza Stazione 47/R, Florence Tel 298841; Autostradale, Piazza Castello 1, Milan Tel 801161

Netherlands: Eurolines, Budget Bus, Rokin 10, Amsterdam Tel 275151

Spain: Linebus, Estacion sur Autobuses, Calle Canarias, Madrid Tel 467265; Julia, Plaza Universidad, Barcelona Tel 3187238

Sweden: GDG Continentbus, Stockholm Tel 234810

Switzerland: Alsa, 13 rue de Fribourg, Geneva Tel 324057

By rail Two companies offering low-cost rail travel in Europe for the under 26's, with a choice of thousands of destinations to many countries in Europe, plus low add-on fares from any UK station, are:

Eurotrain/London Student Travel, 52 Grosvenor Gardens, London SW1W 0AG Tel 01-730 6525, and local offices.

Transalpino, 71-75 Buckingham Palace Road, London SW1W 0QL Tel 01-834 9656, and local offices.

Both issue BIGE tickets, which are available to anyone aged under 26 and offer savings of up to 50% on normal rail fares to Europe. There are lower fares for children under 14 and on some routes for children under 16. The tickets can only be booked through specialised rail travel operators or through appointed student and youth travel offices. BIGE tickets are valid for two months and stop-overs are possible en route. Destinations include Austria, Belgium, Czechoslovakia, Denmark, France, Federal Republic of Germany, Greece, Ireland, Italy, Morocco, Netherlands, Poland, Portugal, Spain, Sweden, Switzerland and Turkey.

Transalpino European representatives are:

Austria: 1 Opernring, Vienna Tel 574495

Belgium: 1A Square du Bastion, Brussels Tel 5111980

Denmark: 6 Skoubogade, Copenhagen Tel 144633

France: 14 Rue Lafayette, Paris Tel 2471240

Federal Republic of Germany: 47 Hohenzollernring, Cologne Tel 20230

Greece: 28 Nikis Street, Athens Tel
20503

Ireland: 24 Talbot Street, Dublin 1
Tel 723825

Italy: 5 Via Locatelli, Milan Tel
6705121

Netherlands: Rokin 44, Amsterdam
Tel 239922

Spain: 9 Plaza de Espana, Madrid
Tel 413478

Sweden: 13 Birger Jarlsgatan,
Stockholm Tel 240710

For details of Eurotrain European
representatives contact the London
office.

For travelling within Britain, anyone
under the age of 24 is entitled to
purchase a British Rail Young
Person's Railcard, entitling the
holder to 50% reduction on day
return tickets, and 33% reduction on
other tickets. The Card costs £12
and is valid for one year. There are
some travel restrictions on certain
routes at peak times. Two recent
passport photographs, plus proof of
age in the form of a birth certificate
or passport are required in order to
obtain a Card. Further details and
application forms are obtainable
from principal British Rail stations
or most student travel offices. British
Rail also offers a variety of discount
tickets depending on your age, the
time of day, the distance you are
travelling etc. Make sure to ask for
the cheapest available ticket when
booking your seat. It is often
cheaper to buy a return ticket than
a single one, but remember to state
how long it will be before you
intend undertaking the return
journey. Further information can be
obtained from British Rail offices or
agents in other countries from any
British Rail station.

By sea Most ferry companies offer
special rates for young people and
groups, and there are often lower
fares for off-peak travel. Details can
be obtained from appointed travel
agents, student travel offices or the
ferry companies themselves.

To give you some idea of the fastest
times of channel crossings:

Felixstowe-Zeebrugge 5hr 15m
Harwich-Hook of Holland 6hr 45m
Sheerness-Vlissingen 7hr
Ramsgate-Dunkerque 1hr 45m
Dover-Oostende 4hr
Dover-Zeebrugge 4hr 30m
Dover-Calais 1hr 15m
Dover-Calais (hovercraft) 30m
Dover-Boulogne 1hr 45m
Dover-Boulogne (hovercraft) 30m
Folkestone-Boulogne 1hr 50m
Newhaven-Dieppe 4hr 15m
Portsmouth-Le Havre 5hr 45m
Portsmouth-Caen 5hr 45m
Portsmouth-Cherbourg 4hr 45m
Portsmouth-St Malo 9hr
Poole-Cherbourg 4hr 30m
Weymouth-Cherbourg 4hr
Plymouth-Roscoff 6hr
Plymouth-Santander 24hr–

By air International air fares and
the regulations covering them
change frequently. It is therefore
advisable to check all possibilities
carefully well in advance. Although
it is worthwhile shopping around, it
is advisable to book only with those
operators/agents who hold an
ATOL (Air Travel Organisers'
Licence). Excursion and Advance
Purchase Excursion (APEX) Fares
have a variety of names depending
on the airline offering them, and
give considerable savings on
normal tickets but impose a variety
of restrictions, such as the time of
purchase before departure, length
of stay on arrival, specific routes,
restricted stop-overs, time of flight
etc. APEX fares are generally
cheaper than excursion fares.

STA Travel, 74 Old Brompton Road, London SW7 3LH Tel 01-581 1022 is one operator specialising in low-cost air travel for young people. Destinations include Australia, Brazil, Canada, Czechoslovakia, Federal Republic of Germany, Greece, Hong Kong, Italy, Portugal, Spain, Switzerland, Turkey and the United States.

Group travel For information and advice on organising group travel independently, the following books are useful:

Help?! - Guidelines on International Youth Exchange, £5.00, available from the Youth Exchange Centre (YEC), Seymour Mews House, Seymour Mews, London W1H 9PE Tel 01-486 5101.

Going Abroad, a practical booklet explaining how to organise an international exchange, with information on funding, travel and administration. Available free from the Scottish Community Education Council (SCEC), Atholl House, 2 Canning Street, Edinburgh EH3 8EG Tel 031-229 2433.

Home and Away, £3.50, a handbook for organising international holidays and exchanges for young people. Available from the Standing Conference of Youth Organisations (SCOYO), 86 Lisburn Road, Belfast BT9 6AF Tel Belfast 681447.

Customs Full details of Customs regulations are given in *United Kingdom Customs (Customs Notice 1)* which is obtainable from HM Customs and Excise or from Customs at ports and airports in the UK. Persons under 17 years of age are not entitled to tobacco or drinks allowances. There are prohibitions and restrictions on the importation of many goods, ranging from drugs and weapons to foodstuffs and plants, and it is therefore advisable

to consult the *Notice* before departure. On arrival in the UK, persons with goods in excess of their duty and tax-free allowances or who are in doubt, should declare the goods in the red clearance channel. For further details, apply to HM Customs and Excise, CDF2, Ground Floor, Dorset House, Stamford Street, London SE1 9PS Tel 01-928 0533 ex 2370/1.

Problems Should you lose your ticket at the last minute, you should contact the airline/shipping company/tour operator immediately to see if a replacement can be issued. If luggage is lost during a flight and does not turn up on arrival at the foreign destination, the duty officer of the airline concerned should be informed immediately. If the luggage cannot be traced, a claim form must be completed. Most airlines will immediately provide a small payment to cover necessities, but they are under no legal obligation to do so, and the amount varies considerably from airline to airline. This payment does not usually have to be repaid if the luggage is traced. If after 3-4 weeks the luggage has still not been found, compensation will be paid by the airline according to the declaration made on the claim form. In any event and to cover loss on other means of transport, it is advisable to take out a personal insurance policy which covers luggage loss. Any losses should of course be reported as soon as possible to the insurance broker concerned.

When you're there You should try to be as friendly and cheerful as possible. If you start off with a positive attitude you will find it much easier to get on with your host family. If you are meeting your exchange partner for the first time, bear in mind that your agency has made every effort to match you according to interests and personality, so you should have a lot of things in common. But don't expect to be best friends from the moment you first meet; it takes time and patience to get to know someone, so make allowances for this. It is only natural that you may feel homesick for the first day or so, especially if you've not been away from home or abroad before. Moping around will not help, and if you phone your parents you may end up missing them even more, not to mention worrying them. The only cure is to put a brave face on it and throw yourself into any activities that your host family are organising. If you are going on a term stay, you should make the most of this by attending school every day. If you are going to be absent for any reason, be sure to get prior permission from your host parents. You could also let your host parents see your report; they are bound to be interested in how you are progressing. It is important to remember that you are a guest in somebody's home, and that your host family is responsible for your welfare during your stay. Their ideas on how young people ought to behave may well differ from those of your parents, but in the interests of harmony you should try to accept them. The agency may also have rules they wish you to follow, and these should be made clear to you beforehand. Consider yourself as an ambassador; your attitudes and behaviour will inevitably influence the impression your host family have of your country.

Code of conduct The following guidelines may be of some help:

Do not go out alone or with friends, even during the day, without first asking permission and explaining where you are going.

Offer to help with the chores, such as clearing the table or washing up.

Create a good impression by clearing up after yourself, keeping your room tidy and making your own bed.

Ask permission before you make any long-distance telephone calls, and pay for them.

Do not smoke or drink alcohol unless you have permission to do so. These habits are usually forbidden by the homestay/ exchange agency in any case.

Be as communicative as possible, even if you are shy. If you don't make the effort your host family will wonder what they've done wrong, it will be unlikely that you will improve your knowledge of the language, and you may all have a miserable time.

Above all, be considerate, helpful and polite.

Food Often you will be asked by the agency to specify any food which you do not like, or which is part of your dietary requirements, beforehand. If there is really something which you do not like, let your host family know, but do remember that learning about new food and customs is an important part of a homestay, so you should try to be open to new ideas and experiences.

Laundry Some host families will be quite willing to do your washing for you, but they are by no means obliged to do so. Guests should check beforehand with their organisation, and also ask permission from the host family if they wish to do some washing for themselves.

Problems A well-organised homestay or exchange should pose few problems. The organisations and agencies in this guide will of course make every effort to ensure that any difficulties which do arise are dealt with quickly and efficiently. Many have local representatives in the host countries, and it is important that you have the address and telephone number of the one nearest to your host family. It is worth clarifying with the organisation what the procedure would be should you find that you wished to terminate the stay earlier than planned. If for example you have made a genuine attempt to overcome difficulties, but still do not get on with your host family, it may be possible for the local representative to arrange alternative accommodation. Where an exchange is involved, the situation becomes more complicated. Should either party feel that they do not wish to complete the second part of the exchange, some kind of mutual agreement will have to be reached concerning payment for hospitality already provided. In some cases it may be possible to find another exchange partner for either or both parties; such negotiations are best handled by the organisation arranging the stay. If you are dissatisfied with the handling of the stay you should put your complaint in writing to the organisation concerned. If you do not receive a satisfactory response, you can, depending on the nature of your complaint, consider the possibility of taking legal advice. Although the Central Bureau cannot accept responsibility for the conduct of an organisation, we would appreciate being informed as soon as possible so that your complaint can be recorded and subsequently investigated. Many of the organisations operating in Britain are members of a regional tourist board. This means that they must ask host families to comply with the British Tourist Authority Code of Conduct with reference to family accommodation. Where problems are encountered it is advisable to inform the relevant tourist board as soon as possible. In case of real emergencies, it is a good idea to have with you addresses and telephone numbers of the relevant embassy or consulate in the country you are going to visit. Details of these can be found under Contact addresses. There are consular offices at British embassies in foreign capitals and at consulates in some provincial cities. Consuls maintain a list of English-speaking doctors and will help in cases of serious difficulties. They cannot give advice on, or pay for, legal proceedings, but will do what they can to help in such cases. As a last resort, a consul can arrange for a direct return to the UK by the cheapest possible passage, providing the individual surrenders their passport and gives a written undertaking to pay the travel expenses involved. The telegraphic address of all British embassies is Prodrome, and of all British consulates Britain, followed in each case by the name of the appropriate town.

Host family guidelines A host family welcomes their visitor not just into their home, but into their life. The guest learns about the family's attitudes and values by participating in its daily routine, while the family learns in turn about the visitor's way of life. If you are considering hosting foreign visitors yourself, and are willing to provide a little more than just accommodation, you should contact an organisation which arranges stays in your area to see if they would be willing to consider you as a host. As the majority of the agencies in this guide specialise in stays for young people, families with children are particularly welcome, since this makes the matching procedure much simpler. However, if you do not have children, or if you wish to receive adult guests, you will still be welcomed by a suitable agency. A representative will visit you in your home, and will need to have details of your family and interests, so that they can match you with a suitable guest. You may find it helpful to talk to other local families who have already hosted a visitor. Many agencies will have guidelines for hosting which they expect you to follow. For example you will probably be requested not to have another guest of the same nationality in the house; this is understandable - guests are there to your language, not to talk in their own. There may also be rules regarding accommodation; in some cases single bedrooms are stipulated. Most guests will appreciate time in their own room occasionally, either to write letters, read, or just rest - it is quite a strain to speak a foreign language all day. It is advisable to abide by the rules laid down by the agency; your guests will be expecting certain standards and may complain to the agency if they find these standards are not being met. Hosting should not be undertaken lightly. It can be very demanding; many agencies expect their families to involve their guests in activities and take them on outings. There should be a genuine desire on your part to welcome a visitor as part of your family; and you should not expect to make a profit, in fact you may well find yourself spending more money than usual while your visitor is with you. However, it is undoubtedly a rewarding experience, and one which many families are happy to repeat.

Preparation If you or your child are to make the first contact with your guest, make sure they receive a cheerful introductory letter in good time. Get the whole family involved in planning activities or outings. Make sure that your guest has a bright, tidy, welcoming room to stay in, with adequate space for clothes. It is important to give your guest a friendly welcome; this is bound to reassure any anxious visitor who may be abroad for the first time. Bear in mind that they may be tired and hungry after their journey and a barrage of questions in a foreign language is not likely to help them relax. A hot drink and bed may be just what they need! For the first day or so they may feel tired, disoriented and possibly homesick. This is perfectly natural, so don't feel that it's due to a failure on your part to make them feel at home. It will soon pass if you keep them occupied and show understanding and affection. Explain to your guest the layout and rules of your household. Don't change your normal family routine just to suit your guest; it is their responsibility to adapt to your way of life, so everyone in the family should just act naturally. You should make allowances for your guest's unfamiliarity with your language. Speak slowly, but avoid colloquial expressions as this will not help them improve their vocabulary. They may sound blunt or rude at times, but this will only be because they don't understand the subtleties of your language yet. Misunderstandings will almost inevitably occur, but treat these with good humour; if your guest can laugh with you at mistakes, then nobody need get embarrassed. Only correct big mistakes; if every little error is corrected your guest will be afraid to talk, whereas encouragement and praise will work wonders. Remember that no matter how intelligent a person is they may feel stupid, shy and cut off when struggling to understand a different language and trying to express their thoughts clearly. Try and involve your guest in every conversation, don't let them feel left out.

Activities You may be surprised what simple things please your guest. You may take for granted something that your guest has never experienced before. Try and think about typically national activities that may interest them. For example in Britain, like riding on the top deck of a double-decker bus or eating fish and chips! Get your guest involved in the discussion, and take their own likes and dislikes into account. They may not be interested in visiting the local museum, but the idea of a picnic on the top of a nearby hill or a trip to the seaside may be more appealing. Don't be afraid to ask their opinion. Treat young guests in general as you would treat your own children. If they are old enough, let them go out on their own as long as this is within the agency's guidelines, but make sure you know where they're going and when they'll be back. Don't take offence if they're keen to go out alone; it's a new experience for them, so try suggesting places they can visit. Make sure they know about public transport, and that they've got your phone number in case they get lost. It probably isn't a good idea though, to give them your house key and let them come and go as they please.

Food Make sure your guest knows the family mealtimes and keeps to them. Eating with the host family is an ideal opportunity for conversation. Do not worry about preparing special foods. Your guest should want to try the national and local specialities, but it is advisable to check for likes and dislikes. You could always offer your guest the opportunity to cook a meal typical of their own country, perhaps as a farewell dinner, and could be a good way for you to find out about their culture.

Other homestays Apart from the homestays already detailed, a number of schemes are in operation whereby one can live and work abroad in a family setting. Very often the work may be on a farm. These programmes should not be classed as holidays, as you are expected to work; they nonetheless offer valuable opportunities for finding out about family life in another country. The following are examples of some of these schemes:

The International Farm Experience Programme provides assistance to young farmers and nurserymen by finding places in farms/nurseries abroad to enable them to broaden their knowledge of agricultural methods. Exchange schemes are operated with Austria, Canada, Denmark, Finland, France, Federal Republic of Germany, Netherlands, Norway, Poland, Sweden, Switzerland and the United States. Applicants live and work with a farmer and his family and the work is matched as far as possible with the applicant's requirements. Ages 18-26. Applicants must have at least 2 years' practical experience, 1 year of which may be at an agricultural college, and intend to make a career in agriculture/horticulture.

The International Agricultural Exchange Association provides opportunities for young agricultural students to acquire practical work experience in the rural sector, and to strengthen and improve their knowledge and understanding of the way of life in other nations. Participants are given an opportunity to study practical methods in other parts of the world on approved training farms, and work as trainees, gaining further experience in their chosen field. Ages 19-28. Applicants should be single, and have good practical experience plus a valid driving licence. Opportunities exist in Australia, New Zealand, Canada and the US for periods of 6-13 months.

For further details of each of the above schemes, apply to the YFC Centre, National Agricultural Centre, Kenilworth, Warwickshire CV8 2LG Tel Coventry 58704

A number of farms provide the opportunity to live and work with an Australian family within a rural and agricultural environment, near rivers, mountains or remote areas of the outback. Participants join in seasonal farming activities such as sheep shearing, cattle mustering/draughting, animal feeding, hay making, crop sowing and harvesting, ploughing, fruit picking butter/flour making and hand milking. Details from the Australian Tourist Commission, Distribution Department, Park Farm Industrial Estate, Park Farm Road, Folkestone, Kent CT19 5DZ.

The English Language Voluntary Organisation, PO Box 32, Basildon, Essex, SS13 3AF was established to promote international communication and friendship, and places students and graduates with Japanese families who provide board and lodging in return for up to 15 hours per week English instruction. The family members wishing to learn English range from young children to adults and instruction tends to be informal; some teaching materials usually supplied. Ages 18+. Applicants must be conscientious and able to adapt to the family's way of life.

English native speakers with A level standard qualifications preferred.

There are opportunities for young people to stay on a farm in Norway as a working guest. Work involves haymaking, weeding, milking, picking fruit, berries and vegetables, tractor driving, feeding cattle, painting, housework and/or taking care of the children, combined with outdoor work. Ages 18-30. Farming experience desirable but not essential. Details from the Norwegian Youth Council, Landsradet for Norske Ungdomsorganisasjoner, Working Guest Programme, Rolf Hofmosgate 18, Oslo 6.

Moshavim are Israeli collectives of individual smallholders, based on the family unit. Each family works and develops its own plot of land/farm while sharing the capital costs of equipment and marketing. Volunteers on moshavim live and work as a member of an Israeli family and are expected to share in the social and cultural activities of the community, and develop close relationships with their family. Most of the work is on the land, with emphasis on flower growing, market gardening and specialist fruit growing. Details of organisations recruiting volunteers and further information is given in *Working Holidays*, the Central Bureau's annual guide to temporary paid and voluntary job opportunities in the UK and over 100 countries overseas.

Working as an au pair is another economical way to spend some time abroad, to study the language, and achieve an awareness of life in another country. An au pair is treated as a member of the family, and in return for board, lodging and pocket money is expected to help with light household duties, including the care of any children, for a maximum of thirty hours per week. There should be sufficient time to make friends, go sightseeing and to take a part-time foreign language course. Further details of British and foreign legislation governing this type of employment, together with addresses of reputable agencies able to arrange placements in countries all over the world are also to be found in *Working Holidays*.

Other exchanges The term exchange can have a very broad meaning, and does not simply refer to the reciprocal visits and stays with families detailed in this guide. There are many types of exchange schemes in operation, covering work experience and observation, study visits and cultural exchanges. Many of the schemes are the result of formal agreements between governments which stipulate a certain number of participants in any given year.

The Central Bureau operates teacher exchange schemes with Austria, Belgium, Denmark, France, the Federal Republic of Germany, Spain, Switzerland, USSR and the US. The schemes are designed for qualified teachers of modern languages and/or related subjects, who currently hold a teaching post, and have a minimum of two years experience. Appointments are for one year, one term or half a term, depending on the country chosen. Teachers exchange posts directly with an overseas colleague and return to their own posts following the exchange. Depending on circumstances, teachers may also wish to swap accommodation for the duration of the exchange.

The Central Bureau also arranges one-way study visits for local education authority administrators, advisers and members of HMI to examine certain aspects of educational provision in another EC country. Grants are available. Reciprocal study visits can be arranged to the United States and Canada for senior administrative staff and headteachers. Participants stay in the homes of their counterparts overseas in return for reciprocal hospitality at a future date.

The Central Bureau is both the UK National Coordinating Agency and a promoting body for the Young Worker Exchange programme sponsored by the European Commission. The main aim of the programme is to enable young people to gain vocational experience and to sample life in another European Community country. There are two types of project: the short term option, 3 weeks-3 months, which offers a programme of meetings and visits focussing on a specific sector of industry or profession in the host country; and the long term option, 4-6+ months, which offers the opportunity to undertake a period of practical work experience in another country. Applicants must be EC nationals between 18 and 28 who have already received some basic vocational training. Knowledge of languages is desirable but not always essential, and language tuition is normally provided in the host country for participants in long term projects.

The International Association For The Exchange Of Students For Technical Experience (IAESTE) runs an exchange scheme providing undergraduate students with course-related industrial, technical or commercial experience in another country. IAESTE covers a wide range of subject fields and operates in North and South America, Europe, the Middle East, Asia and Australia.

Placements last from 8-12 weeks to 1 year. Students pay their own travel expenses; a salary is paid by the firm. Students should apply to their own university or college, which must be affiliated to IAESTE-UK, or they can be nominated by a British company which is sponsoring them on a sandwich course and which must offer a reciprocal placement to an incoming foreign student.

The British Universities Transatlantic Exchanges Committee (BUTEC) and Colleges And Polytechnics Transatlantic Exchanges Committee (CAPTEC) are membership associations of UK higher education institutions with mutual objectives in developing contacts between the UK and the US and Canada through encouragement of staff and student exchange and interchange.

Details of all the above schemes are available from the Central Bureau, Seymour Mews House, Seymour Mews, London W1H 9PE.

The Youth Exchange Centre was established in 1985 by the British Government to promote youth exchanges between the UK and other countries. Its activities fall into the following categories:
Grants; available to British youth groups to assist with the costs not only of travelling abroad, but also of hosting visiting youth groups to the UK. Priority is given to groups of young people, aged 16-25, engaged in two-way exchange projects emphasising social contact with the partner groups. Special funds are reserved for disadvantaged groups of young people such as the unemployed or handicapped. To receive support, exchanges should be designed to increase international understanding and aid the social and cultural development of young people.

Training for Youth Workers. The Centre seeks to improve the quality of international youth exchanges by organising training courses, study visits and placements in the UK and in other countries around particular themes. In cooperation with the Franco-German Youth Office a tri-national programme is underway to develop a greater understanding of internationalism in youth work. A young youth worker exchange is also undertaken with the US.
Information and advice. Special emphasis is placed on providing an information service for all those involved in setting up and running international exchange projects. Much relevant information is contained in the Youth Exchange Centre's publication *Help?!* - see the group travel section of Practical information.
For further details of any of these programmes, contact the Youth Exchange Centre, Seymour Mews House, Seymour Mews, London W1H 9PE.

School and class links A school link is a twinning between two schools in different countries. The teachers responsible for the link organise activities of various kinds which enable the pupils to learn about each other's country and way of life through personal contact. This very often starts with pupils exchanging letters and frequently leads to exchange visits, both individually and in groups. A class link is a twinning between two classes where correspondence and exchange projects can be used to enrich the curriculum, particularly where subjects such as European and world studies, history and geography, and of course modern languages are concerned. Under the guidance of a teacher a class or a group might exchange letters, photographs, audio and video cassettes, joint project work and all types of educational material with

classes in schools abroad.
Penfriend links between individual pupils can also be established, the teachers in charge matching pupils ages and interests. Links involving modern languages in particular frequently lead to exchange visits, either as a group or individually. British links with English-speaking countries, for example the United States, are useful in developing pupils' practical ability to express themselves in their own language, as well as providing an invaluable opportunity to explore a new culture.

School exchanges Generally speaking, the aim of school exchanges is to increase knowledge and understanding of the way of life and culture of other countries. The benefits both to the individual and to the school as a whole, can be both stimulating and enriching, widening the students' horizons and encouraging them to explore and share special interests such as music and sports.

The Central Bureau can, with the cooperation of Ministries of Education abroad, find suitable partner schools for those in the UK wishing to set up a link. Such links can provide a framework for contact in several subject areas and at a variety of levels. Links with countries whose language is taught in British schools (France, Federal Republic of Germany, Austria, Belgium, Italy and Spain) are especially popular, but the Central Bureau also has requests for links from classes in other EC countries, Scandinavia, Eastern Europe and the United States.

Penfriend links The Central Bureau can help find penfriends for individuals between the ages of 8 and 18, in France, the Federal Republic of Germany, Italy, Spain and many other countries. Requests from Scotland should be sent to the Central Bureau's office in Edinburgh; all other requests should be addressed to the Belfast office. See page 2 for addresses.

Local authority and community links There can be financial, organisational and other advantages if group links form part of a broader exchange such as can be provided by a partnership or twinning between towns, districts or counties. The Joint Twinning Committee of the Local Authority Associations, 65 Davies Street, London W1Y 2AA Tel 01-499 8011 maintains a register of civic twinnings and can offer help and advice to local authorities and twinning associations seeking partners abroad. Educational links have also been established by education departments of local authorities. The link may be beased on an existing civic twinning or on the initiative of education officers, groups of teachers or youth leaders who have sought a relevant linking partner.

Home exchanges The idea of exchanging homes, either for a holiday or for longer periods of time, is becoming increasingly popular. Several agencies produce directories giving details of homes which are available for exchange. The advantages of such an arrangement are clear: it provides the opportunity to enjoy low-cost accommodation in a foreign country, without the worry of leaving your own home empty while you are away. Although there can be problems associated with this, the agency should be able to advise on sensible precautions to take. Further details, together with a list of agencies which can arrange home exchanges, are available from the British Tourist Authority, Thames Tower, Black's Road, Hammersmith, London W6 9EL.

Contact addresses

AUSTRALIA

British Consulate General, Commonwealth Avenue, Canberra, ACT 2600

British Council, Edgecliff Centre, 203/233 New South Head Road, Edgecliff, NSW 2027 Tel 326 2022

British Tourist Authority, 4th Floor, Midland House, Clarence Street, Sydney NSW 2000 Tel 2 29 8627

AUSTRIA

British Embassy, Reisnerstrasse 40, 1030 Vienna

British Council, Schenkenstrasse 4, 1010 Vienna Tel 63 26 16

BELGIUM

British Embassy, Britannia House, rue Joseph II 28, 1040 Brussels

British Council, Britannia House, 30 rue Joseph II, 1040 Brussels Tel 2 19 36 00

British Tourist Authority, 52 Rue de la Montagne, 1000 Brussels Tel 2 511 4390

BRAZIL

British Council, CRN 708/9-B1 3 Nos 1/3, 70.740 Brasilia DF Tel 272 3060

British Tourist Authority, Avenida Ipiranga 318-A, 12. Andar, Conjunto 1201, Edificio Vila Normanda, 01046 Sao Paulo SP Tel 11 257 1834

BRITAIN

Australian Tourist Commission, 4th Floor, Heathcoat House, 20 Savile Row, London W1X 1AE Tel 01-434 4371

Austrian Embassy, 18 Belgrave Mews West, London SW1X 8HU Tel 01-235 3731

Austrian National Tourist Office, 30 St George Street, London W1R 9FA Tel 01-629 0461

Belgian Embassy, 103 Eaton Square, London SW1W 9AB Tel 01-235 5422

Belgian National Tourist Office, 38 Dover Street, London W1X 3RB Tel 01-499 5379

Brazilian Embassy, 32 Green Street, Mayfair, London W1Y 4AT Tel 01-499 0877

Canadian High Commission, Canada House, Trafalgar Square, London SW1Y 5BJ Tel 01-930 9741

Tourism Canada, PO Box 9, London SW1Y 5DR Tel 01-629 9492

Czechoslovak Embassy, 25 Kensington Palace Gardens, London W8 4QY Tel 01-229 1255

Cedok (Czechoslovakia), 17-18 Old Bond Street, London W1X 3DA Tel 01-629 6058

Royal Danish Embassy, 55 Sloane Street, London SW1X 9SR Tel 01-235 1255

Danish Tourist Board, Sceptre House, 169/173 Regent Street, London W1R 8PY Tel 01-734 2637

Egyptian Embassy, 26 South Street, London W1Y 8EL Tel 01-449 2401

Egyptian State Tourist Centre, 168 Piccadilly, London W1V 9HL Tel 01-493 5282

French Embassy, 58 Knightsbridge, London SW1X 7JT Tel 01-235 8080

French Government Tourist Office, 178 Piccadilly, London W1V 0AL Tel 01-491 7622

Embassy of the Federal Republic of Germany, 23 Belgrave Square, London SW1X 8PZ Tel 01-235 5033

German National Tourist Office, 61 Conduit Street, London W1R 0EN Tel 01-734 2600

Greek Embassy, 1A Holland Park, London W11 3TP Tel 01-727 8040

National Tourist Organisation of Greece, 195-197 Regent Street, London W1R 8DL Tel 01-734 5997

Indonesian Embassy, 38 Grosvenor Square, London W1X 9AD Tel 01-499 7661

Irish Embassy, 17 Grosvenor Place, London SW1X 7HR Tel 01-235 2171

Irish Tourist Office, Ireland House, 150 New Bond Street, London W1Y 0AQ Tel 01-493 3201

Italian Consulate General, 38 Eaton Place, London SW1X 8AN Tel 01-235 9371

Italian State Tourist Office, 1 Princes Street, London W1R 8AY Tel 01-408 1254

Japanese Embassy, 46 Grosvenor Street, London W1X 0BA Tel 01-493 6030

Japanese National Tourist Organisation, 167 Regent Street, London W1R 7FD Tel 01-734 9638

Korean Embassy, 4 Palace Gate, London W8 5NF Tel 01-581 0247

Malta High Commission, 16 Kensingtnon Square, London W8 5HH Tel 01-938 1712

Malta National Tourist Organisation, 207 College House, Wrights Lane, London W8 5SH Tel 01-938 2668

Mexican Ministry for Tourism, 7 Cork Street, London W1X 1PB Tel 01-734 1058

Netherlands Embassy, 38 Hyde Park Gate, London SW7 5DP Tel 01-584 5040

Netherlands Board of Tourism, 25-28 Buckingham Gate, London SW1E 6LD Tel 01-630 0451

New Zealand High Commission, New Zealand House, 80 Haymarket, London SW1Y 4TQ Tel 01-930 8422

Polish Embassy, 47 Portland Place, London W1N 3AG Tel 01-580 4324

Polorbis Travel Ltd, 82 Mortimer Street, London W1N 7DE Tel 01-637 4971

Portuguese Embassy, 11 Belgrave Square, London SW1X 8PP Tel 01-235 5331

Portuguese National Tourist Office, New Bond House, 1/5 New Bond Street, London W1Y 0NP Tel 01-493 3873

Spanish Embassy, 24 Belgrave Square, London SW1X 8QA Tel 01-235 1484

Spanish National Tourist Office, 57/58 St James's Street, London SW1 Tel 01-499 0901

Swedish Embassy, 11 Montagu Place, London W1H 2AL Tel 01-724 2101

Swedish National Tourist Office, 3 Cork Street, London W1X 1HA Tel 01-437 5816

Swiss Embassy, 16/18 Montagu Place, London W1H 2BQ Tel 01-723 0701

Swiss National Tourist Office, Swiss Centre, 1 New Coventry Street, London W1V 3HG Tel 01-734 1921

Turkish Consulate General, Rutland Lodge, Rutland Gardens, London SW7 1BW Tel 01-589 0360

US Embassy, 24 Grosvenor Square, London W1A 2JB Tel 01-499 7010

United States Travel and Tourism, Administration, 22 Sackville Street, London W1X 2EA Tel 01-439 7433

CANADA

British High Commission, 80 Elgin Street, Ottowa, Ontario K1P 5K7

British Council c/o British High Commission

British Tourist Authority, 94 Cumberland Street, Suite 600, Toronto, Ontario M5R 3N3 Tel 416 961 8124

CZECHOSLOVAKIA

British Embassy, 110 00 Jungmannova 30, Prague 1 Tel 22 45 01

British Council c/o British Embassy

DENMARK

British Embassy, Kastelsvej 38/40, 2100 Copenhagen 0

British Council, Montergade 1, 1116 Copenhagen K Tel 11 20 44

British Tourist Authority, Montergade 3, 1116 Copenhagen K Tel 1 12 07 93

EGYPT

British Embassy, Ahmed, Ragheb Street, Cairo City, Cairo

British Council, 192 Sharia el Nil, Agouza, Cairo Tel 3460577

FRANCE

British Embassy, 35 rue de Faubourg St Honore, 75008 Paris

British Council, 9 rue de Constantine, 75007 Paris Tel 45 55 95 95

British Tourist Authority, 63 rue Pierre Charron, 75008 Paris Tel 42 89 11 11

FEDERAL REPUBLIC OF GERMANY

British Embassy, Friedrich-Ebert Allee 77, 5300 Bonn

British Council, Hahnenstrasse 6, 5000 Cologne 1 Tel 23 66 77

British Tourist Authority, Neue Mainzer Strasse 22, 6000 Frankfurt 1 Tel 23 807 50

GREECE

British Embassy, 1 Ploutarchou Street, Athens

British Council, 17 Plateia Philikis Etairias, Kolonaki Square, 106/73 Athens Tel 3633211

HONG KONG

British Council, Easey Commercial Building, 255 Hennessy Road, Wanchai

British Tourist Authority, Suite 903, 1 Hysan Avenue, Causeway Bay

IRELAND

British Embassy, 33 Merrion Road, Dublin 4, Tel: 695211

British Tourist Authority c/o British Airways, 112 Grafton Street, Dublin 2

ITALY

British Embassy, Via XX Settembre 80A, 00187 Rome

British Council, Palazzo del Drago, Via Quattro Fontane 20, 00184 Rome

British Tourist Authority, Via S Eufemia 5, 00187 Rome Tel 678 55 48

JAPAN

British Council, 2-Kagurazaka 1-Chome, Shinjuku-ku, Tokyo 162

British Embassy, 1 Ichiban-cho, Chiyoda-ku, Tokyo

British Tourist Authority, Tokyo Club Building (Room 246), 3-2-6 Kasumigaseki, Chiyoda-Ku, Tokyo 100 Tel 581 3603

MALTA

British High Commission, 7 St Anne Street, Floriana

MEXICO

British Embassy, Rio Lerma 71, Cuauhtemoc, 06500 Mexico DF

British Council, Maestro Antonio Caso 127, Col. San Rafael, Mexico 06470 DF Tel 566 61 44

British Tourist Authority, c/o Embajada Britanica, Edificio Alber, Paseo de la Reforma 332 - 5. Piso, Mexico 06600 DF Tel 533 6375

NETHERLANDS

British Embassy, Lange Voorhout 10, 2514 ED The Hague

British Council, Keizersgracht 343, 1016 EH Amsterdam Tel 223644

British Tourist Authority, Aurora Gebouw (5e), Stadhouderskade 2, 1054 ES Amsterdam Tel 855051

NEW ZEALAND

British High Commission, Reserve Bank Building, 2 The Terrace, PO Box 1812, Wellington 1

British Council c/o British High Commission

POLAND

British Embassy, Aleja Roz 1, 00-556 Warsaw

British Council, Al Jerozolimskie 59, 00-697 Warsaw Tel 287401

PORTUGAL

British Embassy, 35/39 Rua S Domingos a Lapa, Lisbon 3

British Council, Rua Cecilio de Sousa 65, 1294 Lisbon Codex Tel 369208

SPAIN

British Embassy, Calle de Fernando El Santo 16, Madrid 4

British Council, Calle Almagro 5, 28001 Madrid Tel 4191250

British Tourist Authority Torre de Madrid 6/4, Plaza de Espana, 28008 Madrid Tel 241 13 96

SWEDEN

British Embassy, Skarpogatan 6, 115 27 Stockholm

British Council, Skarpogatan 6, 115-27 Stockholm Tel 670 140

British Tourist Authority, Malmskillnadsgatan 42 (1st Floor), 11157 Stockholm Tel 21 42 52

SWITZERLAND

British Embassy, Thunstrasse 50, 3005 Bern

British Tourist Authority, Limmatquai 78, 8001 Zurich Tel 47 42 77

TURKEY

British Embassy, Sehit Ersan Caddesi 46/A, Cankaya, Ankara

British Council, 50-52 Guniz Sokak, Kavaklidere, Ankara Tel 28 31 65

UNITED STATES

British Embassy, 3100 Massachusetts Avenue NW, Washington DC 20008

British Council, c/o British Embassy

British Tourist Authority, 3rd Floor, 40 West 57th Street, New York NY 10019, Tel: 581 4700; John Hancock Centre, Suite 3320, 875 North Michigan Avenue, Chicago, Illinois, Tel: 787 0490

REPORT FORM

HOME FROM HOME REPORT FORM

Name and address of organisation(s) concerned

Homestay, exchange or term stay?

Country/countries visited

Length and dates of stay

Was correspondence prompt and satisfactory?

Were the matching arrangements successful?

Were you satisfied with the financial arrangements?

Were travel arrangements efficient?

Were the accommodation and meals satisfactory?

Were you satisfied with the planning of the visit?

Would you recommend this homestay/exchange and the organisation to other people?

What were the ages of the participants?

Any other comments:

Signed

Date

Name

Address